"Merry c...
opened the...
a mischievo...

"Merry Chr... ...sit answered, smiling a
small, nervous smile as she admired his broad
shoulders covered in a black cashmere topcoat.
The blood of mistletoe over her face when he
held a sprig to kiss her. He simply touched his
leaned down to hers, but even that brief contact had
mouth to hers, but even that brief contact had
her brain short-circuiting.

"Do you want to try for 'Happy New Year'?"
Nick asked teasingly," she echoed softly. At that
"Happy New Year," and this time the fierce
his lips met hers again, and this time the fierce
pleasure of his caress tingled all the way to her
toes.

"What next," he asked. "Groundhog Day?"
Dovie bubbled with laughter as he tossed the
sprig of mistletoe over his shoulder and opened
arms to her, giving her a brief glimpse of
a black tuxedo that made him look like a
... in GQ.

"... she murmured. "Happy
... ck."
... sting silk and rapid
... in warm cashmere
... ling lips Dovie
... Day, I can

LOVESWEPT® • 161

Fran Baker
Seeing Stars

 BANTAM BOOKS
TORONTO • NEW YORK • LONDON • SYDNEY • AUCKLAND

SEEING STARS

A Bantam Book / October 1986

Published simultaneously in the United States and Canada

Bantam Books are published by Bantam Books, Inc. Its trade-
mark, consisting of the words "Bantam Books" and the por-
trayal of a rooster, is Registered in U.S. Patent and Trademark
Office and in other countries. Marca Registrada. Bantam
Books, Inc., 666 Fifth Avenue, New York, New York 10103.

PRINTED IN THE UNITED STATES OF AMERICA

O   0 9 8 7 6 5 4 3 2 1

Thanx, Pat

One

Darn!

Dovie stopped at the foot of Spicey Hill, her spirits and the tip of her fly rod sinking in tandem when she saw the fisherman.

What rotten luck . . . not only had some Johnny-come-lately commandeered her favorite spot at the river's bend, but, judging from the way his line just went taut, he'd also caught her Christmas dinner!

He played it so perfectly, though, even reeling backward at times, that she couldn't help but admire his skill.

And when the trout made a futile attempt to turn downriver against the toughest rod pressure she'd ever seen applied, Dovie had to admit that the man could probably fish rings around her, four days out of seven.

"Careful," she cautioned softly when he started

down the steeply sloped bank toward the water's edge.

She didn't want to distract him; a trout that big could break free in the blink of an eye. But the riverbed was so littered with rocks this time of year, he'd be well advised to look before he leaped. She couldn't swim, and the closest doctor was in Richmond—an hour's drive away.

Surely he'll see them, Dovie thought, frustrated because *she* suddenly couldn't see a blessed thing from where she stood.

Curiosity killed the cat, she reminded herself glumly as she took a few cautious steps forward. But satisfaction brought it back! She rejoiced as she got a better grip on her fly rod and broke into a run toward the riverbank. Heckfire. She'd landed that trout a thousand times in her dreams, and she sure wanted to be front and center for the real thing!

All at once the trout turned and streaked upstream, stretching the fisherman's line as long and straight as hot, sticky taffy being pulled. The tip of his rod snapped down past his knees, bending in a thin fiberglass horseshoe, and Dovie knew he had a bona fide fight on his hands.

He brought the rod tip up and tightened the drag of his reel. Then he lunged into the cold, churning water and began stalking the trout with a savvy that seemed born of experience. Surprisingly, he never looked down. He simply tested the riverbed for rocks with the toe of his wader boot before taking each step.

Around and round they went. And it was exhausting yet exhilarating to watch. Two worthy opponents linked in a life-and-death struggle that came to a stunning conclusion.

Dovie watched transfixed as the trout jumped high in the air. It shook the lure embedded in its mouth while flinging drops of liquid silver water against the somber December sky, then jackknifed back into the water.

A lesser fisherman would have lost it then and there.

But when *this* man reared back and reeled hard, she suddenly became aware of how strong he must be, how the muscles in his arms and shoulders tautened like sinuous thongs beneath his chamois-cloth shirt.

In the tremulous winter light Dovie could almost see him three hundred summers ago: the noble savage, naked but for a loincloth. Leading his warriors into battle at the crack of dawn. Bedding his woman by a brilliant Shenandoah moon.

She laughed self-consciously at her own imagery.

The object of that imagery turned his head, as though he'd heard her laughing over the trill of the rapids, and she found herself really looking at him for the first time.

His windblown black hair framed a face that had weathered fortune's hurricane with flint and style.

The high, spare cheekbones bore a few faint scars; that machete of a nose had been broken at least once; and the wide mouth mocked convention in a way that both frightened and fascinated her.

Dovie couldn't tell what color his eyes were behind the large opaque sunglasses he wore, but she would have bet her bottom dollar they were blue. She didn't know why she felt so certain about it, or, for that matter, why she should even care. But she did.

Without so much as a "how do you do" he turned his attention back to the trout. She stood on the bank, mulling over a tiny stab of—what? Disappointment? How absurd! He was a stranger, for heaven's sake. Chances were she'd never see him again. And yet something within her craved his notice.

"Atta boy," he crooned as the trout began swimming in small, tight circles directly in front of him, fanning its tail as though admitting defeat. "Come on home."

His vibrant baritone voice enveloped her as gently as an embrace. Dovie shivered despite the warm woolen shirt she wore, and wondered if she was getting addlepated in her old age.

Not that she equated turning thirty-five on her next birthday with being over the hill. It was just that there were times when she would have loved to share the joy of the simpler things in life with someone special. Her joy at finally seeing the trout, for example.

"Okay, big fella . . ." He urged the trout toward shore, and it was finally tired enough to go along. And when he dipped his arms in up to the elbows and lifted it out of the water, Dovie couldn't take her eyes off it.

A beautiful rainbow—five, maybe six pounds—with a thick, streamlined flank. Its gills moved in and out, feeding its strength, as the fisherman cradled it in his large, capable hands.

He took the hook from its mouth, his supple fingers working swiftly but tenderly, and tears clustered in her throat when a trace of blood trickled from the corner of its jaw, to be carried away by the current.

It was more magnificent than any trout she'd ever even hoped existed in these icy waters . . . its iridescent body contrasting with a belly the color of fresh cream . . . its velvety sides heaving in exhaustion. And more than anything on God's good earth, she wanted him to let it live.

As if he'd read her mind, the fisherman laid his fly rod on the bank and waded out into the river. And when he lowered the trout into the water and opened his hands, it shot away like a bullet.

He threw his head back then and laughed, a mellow sound that made her think all the fun in the world had lodged in his chest and was trying to break free . . . and she was smitten on the spot.

Dovie stood dumbfounded. His laughter had touched a part of her that she'd thought had atrophied from disuse a long time ago. But as she stared at his powerful body, silhouetted against the steely sky, that same part of her suddenly ached to be touched again.

He wheeled and started back to the bank, still testing the riverbed for rocks with the toe of his wader boot.

Frantically she racked her brain for something reasonably intelligent to say to him by way of introduction.

He stopped, whipped off his dark glasses, and dried his sun-bronzed face on his shirt sleeve. The wind tossed his black hair, making him look wild and reckless and totally male.

Frustrated by the small delay, she stamped her foot. The bank was slick and damp and steep. She slipped and, too startled even to scream for help, fell into the freezing water.

His head snapped up as if the trap door of a gallows had opened beneath his feet.

Right before the river of darkness engulfed her, Dovie saw his eyes. Blue as water. Bleak as winter.

"What the hell—?"

A million icy needles hit Nick full in the face. He spit out a mouthful of slushy water, totally baffled by what had caused such a big splash. Cursing silently but eloquently now, he reached up to rake back the sodden strands of hair that had fallen into his eyes, and halted in mid-action.

His sunglasses were gone.

Angrily he began groping around in the bone-chilling water, trying to find them before he stepped on them.

There. What was that?

His fingers closed on a firm, round breast, and his mood went from bad to worse when he realized that he'd overlooked the obvious reason for that splash: The woman with the low, malty laugh had fallen into the river!

"Son of a—" Biting off the oath of utter self-disgust, he gathered her inert figure into his arms and carried her unerringly to the bank. When he laid her on the ground she choked up the water she'd swallowed and drew a shuddering gasp of air, her first since he'd found her.

Nick crouched beside her and checked her vital signs. Respiration shallow, pulse rapid but weak—symptoms of shock. Playing it safe, he also examined her neck and skull. No bumps or palpable fractures to indicate a head injury of any sort.

She was soaked to the skin and shaking so hard that he could feel the vibrations where his knees touched the ground. Having treated dozens of hypothermia victims in his day, he knew he'd better get her into some warm, dry clothes immediately.

Careful not to disturb her any more than necessary, he slipped the straps of her rubber waders off her narrow shoulders, then peeled the unwieldy things down her short but shapely legs and pulled them over her small, booted feet. The water that her jeans and shirt hadn't already absorbed rushed onto his hands in a freezing cascade.

That done, he shucked his own waders and undressed to his thermal underwear. Then, using his own body as both brace and windbreak, he propped her limp form into a sitting position, unbuttoned her wet wool shirt, and slid the sleeves off her arms.

She had a delicate bone structure despite her hourglass shape, something Nick couldn't help but notice as he clasped her graceful rib cage with one hand while removing her damp cotton bra with the other. The blood surged to his head when her generous breasts finally spilled free, and he clamped down a highly unprofessional urge to stroke their satiny undersides.

Gut instinct warned him to get this done quickly and get the hell out of there. Her head lolled as trustingly as a child's against his chest, and his arm tightened possessively, protectively, for a traitorous heartbeat before he set her firmly away from him.

He'd already lost everything else. Damned if he was going to lose his fool head over some Barbie doll who'd practically fallen into his lap!

Back to the business at hand, he put his shirt on her and buttoned it to her neck against the piercing cold. His fingers lacked their usual dexterity, but then, it had been a while since he'd dressed a woman. Or *undressed* one, he reminded himself wryly.

All right, you dumb son of a gun, *you* started this. . . . He reached for the snap at her wasp-thin waist, remembered he'd forgotten to remove her boots, and bent to the task as gratefully as a condemned man granted a stay of execution. Her soggy knee socks then went the way of her boots.

Strictly by rote he rubbed her bare feet to stimulate her circulation. When he kneaded her ticklish soles, ten tiny toes curled reflexively in his palm. Amusement ripened the ironical smile on his lips as his sensitive fingers followed the pedial lines upward, to ankles so daintily boned he could have crushed them with his bare hands.

He caressed them instead. Her breath came out in a raspy sigh that played counterpoint to his rapidly escalating pulse. He dropped her feet as if they'd suddenly become too hot to handle, and her heels hit the bank with a dull thud.

Dear Lord, why had he gotten involved in this anyway? Nick raised his forearm to wipe the cold sweat off his brow, and his mouth tensed into a grim line when he remembered his missing sunglasses. It never paid to play the Good Samaritan. He should have learned that by now!

Having gone this far, though, he was determined to see it through. The zipper of her jeans parted with a frostbitten protest. He drew the wet denim down her sweetly flared hips and slender thighs, over her slightly knocked knees, shapely calves, and finely arched feet. He hesitated only an instant before peeling off her panties and tossing them aside too.

She moaned, alerting him to the fact she was finally coming around.

Nick knew he'd better get this done before she realized she was naked from the waist down and started screaming bloody murder.

Damn! If only he could slip into her subconscious mind for a moment and . . . What the hell, it was worth a try.

"Listen, lady, I'm a doctor," he stated with more confidence then he'd felt in a year. His fingers circled her slim ankle as he prodded her memory. "You fell in the river—remember?—and I pulled you out."

She sighed as if to say she'd heard him.

"Well, I'm right in the middle of changing your clothes and . . ." His hand grazed her smooth calf muscle, and he wished to high heaven that she didn't feel so good.

As though she'd divined the direction of his thoughts, she groaned and locked her legs together.

"Sorry." Mentally cursing himself for the lapse, Nick slid his hand back to her ankle, treating it as neutral territory, and promised softly, "That won't happen again—I swear it."

When her muscles and the meter of her breathing relaxed, he resumed speaking in normal conversational tones. "Now, the next thing you're going to feel is just me putting my jeans on you."

There were more words. Inconsequential words. The important thing was, she didn't fight him when he pulled his dry Levis on over her feet. Or her calves. Or her knees. But when he reached her silky thighs, she suddenly pushed his hands away and rolled sideways.

"Wait! I'm a doctor, remember?" He reached to roll her body back. "Besides, I won't see anything I shouldn't, because—"

Pain cracked through his head as the palm of her small hand connected smartly with his cheek.

"Well, I'll be damned!" The aggressive side of Nick's nature abruptly reasserted itself as he forced her down and straddled her legs. When she swung at him a second time—with both hands, no less—he sensed it coming and caught her wrists, imprisoning them above her head in his iron fists.

"Let me go!" she ordered, gasping.

"*Look*, lady"—he smiled coldly at his choice of words and spat the bitter truth at her through clenched teeth—"I'm *blind*!"

Two

Dovie stared at him in disbelief. She was so close, she could see every line in his burnished skin, every scar that should have lessened his appeal but didn't, and every spiky black lash defining those deep blue eyes that seemed to look into infinity. . . .

"How did you get me back to the bank?" The instant the words left her mouth, Dovie wanted to bite her tongue. Just because he couldn't see didn't mean he couldn't do anything else!

"I'm not totally inadequate," Nick retorted. And nothing riled him more than someone implying otherwise.

"I—I didn't say you were." Embarrassed to think he'd taken her question the wrong way, she tried to make amends. "I'm impressed. Really! I mean, I can't even swim, and here you—"

"Spare me the platitudes," he snapped.

Of all the pompous, self-pitying . . . Irritated that she was paying for something that was none of her doing, she shot back with, "It could be worse."

"Oh, sure." He breathed out a short laugh that lacked humor. "I could be a blind eunuch."

Dovie sucked in a shocked lungful of air, suddenly aware of his heat and his hardness pinning her partially nude body to the cold ground. The tightly waffled knit of his long underwear clung so snugly to his lean torso that it left nothing to her imagination. Not even the fact that he'd begun to desire her . . .

When she shifted nervously beneath him Nick gritted his teeth, trying valiantly to ignore the voluptuous press of her breasts against his chest and the sweet promise of her hips against his. But after the long months of abstinence, there was a limit to what a man could take!

The silence was pregnant enough to bear twins.

She lay still, afraid to move again, sensing she'd aroused a sleeping tiger that nothing in her experience had prepared her to tame. He raised one eyebrow, as if the notion of having her at his mercy appealed to him, and a rage she'd never known she was capable of shook her from head to toe. Damn him for putting her on the defensive!

"Get off of me," she ordered sharply.

"Gladly," he said, and groaned.

But instead of being relieved when he released her wrists and pushed lithely to his feet, Dovie felt a perverse sense of loss. And when she saw the dark red imprint of her fingers against his face, she really wished she hadn't slapped him that hard. After all, he'd only been trying to help.

"I haven't thanked you yet for saving me," she said, remembering suddenly. Law, he must think her a real ingrate!

Doing his best to disguise the unfortunate physical effect she'd had on him, Nick shrugged off her gratitude and geared up for a lecture. Little idiot had it coming! "Why weren't you wearing a life jacket?"

"I don't own one." Was it her fault that every time she had an extra dime to her name, someone in her family needed it more than she did?

"You can't swim and you don't own a life jacket." His derisive expression spoke volumes. "Lady, you're an accident looking for a place to happen."

"No, I'm not!" Dovie jumped to her feet so fast and furiously that her jeans—his jeans, rather— fell down around her ankles with a soft *whoosh*.

A mischievous smile shunted across his alluring mouth when he heard her pants drop. "Do my ears deceive me or are you trussed up tighter than a Christmas turkey right now?"

"Gobble, gobble!" she snapped, in no mood to be patronized. Least of all by him!

Like sunshine after rain, his laughter cleared the air between them, and she caught herself basking in the rich, welcome warmth of it.

"Ask a stupid question . . ." Dovie quipped, smiling as she reached down to pull up her pants.

The numbing air nipped at her bare backside, and she thought how cold he must be with only his long johns to protect him. "Which reminds me, the least I can do is offer the man who rescued me a cup of coffee."

"The man who rescued you is named Nick Monroe." He rubbed those strong but compassionate hands together briskly, trying to warm them. "And I'd give my eyeteeth for a cup of hot coffee."

"Pleased to meet you, Nick, although I can't say much for the circumstances." Holding the waistband of her borrowed jeans securely in place with one hand, she squeezed icy water out of her hair with the other. "I'm Dovie Brown."

"Dovie." His deep voice breathed such luxuriant new life into her old-fashioned name that it melted the very marrow of her bones.

And when he reached out and caught her wrist, drawing her closer and asking, "Let me see what you look like," she couldn't have denied him had her life depended on it.

The blood rushed to her head, a dizzying high, as he ran his long fingers through the short, damp layers of her hair. He brushed it this way and that, seemingly fascinated by the take-it-or-leave-it simplicity of style and its tendency to wave as it dried.

"I'll bet it's brown."

"How did you know?"

"Actually, it was a pretty safe bet." Nick slid his hand around to her satiny nape, twining his thumb in the lowest hairs. "About half of the population has hair that's some shade of brown."

"Do tell." Shivers of delight winged along her spine when his fingers followed her hairline from the base of her skull to the shell of her ear.

"Mm-hmmm." He lifted a damp tendril of hair from her cheek, marveling at its feathery-fine texture. "Light or dark?"

"Dark." Her eyelids drifted closed as his searching fingers traced their slightly tip-tilted shape, leaving a faint erotic glow in their wake.

"And your eyes?" Pain and longing such as he'd never experienced before twisted his gut. What he wouldn't give, just this once, to see them sparkling with laughter or smoldering with passion!

"The same, dark brown." Dovie tensed when Nick's hands came up to frame her face between his palms. She'd held up pretty well, considering, and she could only hope that he wasn't disappointed by what he was "seeing."

"Beautiful," he murmured reverently as he contoured the classic rise of her cheekbones, the narrow slope of her nose, and the bewitching curve of her mouth.

Dovie could hardly believe her ears. Her parents had always called her "dependable," and she'd done everything in her power to prove them right. Friends and relations generally relied on her when they needed a favor. Her nieces and nephews had gifted her with the nickname "Aunt Granny." But neither kith nor kin had ever called her—

"Beautiful," he repeated huskily, rubbing the tip of his forefinger back and forth across her lower lip. Feeling her breath on the top of his finger and her warm skin beneath, he was tempted . . . oh, so tempted.

Eyes closed and lips primed by the exquisite friction of Nick's finger, Dovie awaited the heat of his kiss with eager dread. She barely knew him, but he'd pushed all the right buttons and opened all her secret doors.

"Look"—he dropped his hands in stringent self-denial—"I didn't mean to embarrass you." Touching her hadn't been a particularly smart move. He knew himself well enough to realize that he'd gone too long without a woman. One kiss wouldn't cut it. And something told him that this woman wasn't into playing games.

"I—" Opening her eyes, only to encounter his frozen expression, Dovie felt chilled clean to the bone. "I don't understand."

"Well, *these* are my eyes now." Nick held out his hands, palms up and fingers splayed, and hot color climbed her cheeks as she remembered that those same hands had removed all her clothing a little while ago.

"And?" Abruptly she felt her old insecurities begin to slip back into place. She was too short . . . too fat . . . too plain.

"And a lot of sighted people are uncomfortable with the idea of a blind person"—his unsmiling face looked as ominous as those storm clouds overhead—"*feeling them up,* for lack of a better phrase."

For long seconds she simply stared at his hands, which were as clean and steady as a surgeon's. Then she went limp with relief when she remembered who he was.

"Why on earth should I be embarrassed?" Dovie asked, as much of herself as of him. "You're a doctor!"

"Not anymore."

"But—"

"But nothing!" Nick said it in a way that told her the topic was closed to further discussion. He reached down, found his socks and waders right where he'd left them, then changed the subject with a curt "Which would you rather wear?"

Dovie had more sense than to beat her head against a stone wall. Besides, the snow that had been threatening all morning had finally begun to fall, and neither one of them was exactly dressed to brave the elements.

"The socks." She took them gingerly, trying to avoid touching him. In spite of her precaution, her fingertips grazed his. The fleeting thrill of flesh against flesh struck nerve endings she hadn't even known she possessed.

"We'd best get a move on," Nick said, every sensory receptor in his body suddenly going like a fire bell. Nothing could come of these feelings, of course, so the sooner he hit the road the better for both of them.

"I suppose," she said, and sighed, knowing he was right but strangely reluctant to admit it aloud.

Silence fell like a hundred-year-old oak, and they were back to square one.

He was insane to go home with her, Nick thought as he pulled on his rubber waders. Especially considering the effect she'd had on him since the first instant her Lorelei laughter had beckoned his imagination.

Belatedly he realized he had his waders on backward. Though his throat worked furiously, not a word passed his lips.

Watching him struggle to get his waders on the right feet, Dovie felt a strong urge to offer her help. It would go so much more quickly if she did! But something—a sixth sense, perhaps—warned her that this muleheaded man would probably rebuff the gesture as rudely as he'd rejected everything else about her.

She slipped on his socks and forced herself to look elsewhere while he finished dressing.

"Where do you live?" He broke the silence at the same time that his tapered fingers began fumbling with the small belt at the waistband of his waders.

"At the top of the hill." She balled her hands into tight fists and pressed them to her sides, fighting to keep from reaching over there to buckle it for him.

"Do you have a telephone?" How the hell could a man who'd sutured thousands of serious lacerations have so much trouble threading a strip of rubber through a piece of plastic? he wondered.

"And electricity, and indoor plumbing . . ." Dovie relaxed her clenched fists when he finally got his belt buckled. The hardest thing she'd ever done was to stand there and do nothing!

"Fine." Cursing himself for a clumsy fool, Nick took a swipe at the delicate snowflake that had dared to land on his badly bent nose. "I'll call my houseman and have him come after me."

"Okay." But the thought of his leaving brought an odd lump to her throat.

The blustery wind tore at his thick black hair, whipping it about his austerely handsome face as he swallowed his pride and sought her help. "Can you point me toward my fly rod?"

"Here—" She started forward, only too glad to get it for him.

"*No!*" Nick's command thundered to the hills and back again, stopping her cold. "Just tell me where it is," he said, "and I'll get it myself."

"Behind you," she whispered, wounded as surely as if he'd slapped her hard. "And a little to your left."

"Thank you." Turning in the direction she'd indicated, he found his fly rod. Damn! He hadn't meant to hurt her feelings, but he'd had his fill of meddlesome strangers.

Seeing as how he was so bent on doing for himself, Dovie pulled back. "You're welcome."

It was more than pride that made him as independent as a hog on ice, she realized as she watched him take his tackle down. He seemed to think he had to justify his existence and prove his worth to every sighted person he met. Maybe all he really needed, she mused, was to be treated normally.

Holding that thought, she turned the tables on him. "Where do *you* live?"

"Richmond." After removing the leader he'd used with his lure, Nick tied the end of his fishing line to the eye at the tip of his fly rod. Soft jubilance lifted his heavy spirit as he made a perfect surgeon's knot. At least he could still do that right!

"Gosh, you sure came far out of your way just to catch a trout and turn it loose." Desperate for something to do with *her* hands, Dovie knelt and began wringing out her wet clothes.

"Sure did," he agreed smoothly, cautious. Some things were better left unsaid. If he told this pint-sized mother hen about that cabin he'd rented a half mile west of here, he'd probably find her camped on his doorstep tomorrow morning oozing chicken soup and sympathy from every pore!

What the heck, Dovie decided, she might as well shoot the works. "Are you married?"

His taciturn profile told her she'd pushed him too far.

She sighed dismally. "I didn't mean to pry."

If she had pressed him, Nick would have remained obdurately silent. But on hearing that sigh followed by the note of regret in her voice, he opened up a little. "I'm divorced."

"I'm sorry." Her apology was no less sincere for its brevity.

"I'm not." The terse denial was rude, and he tried to soften his words. "It happened a couple of years before I went blind, so there's no sense in your thinking I was abandoned in my hour of need."

He took up the slack in his line, then locked his reel, so it wouldn't spin loose. "Are you—"

"No," she interrupted rashly. "I've never been married."

"—*ready to go?*" he finished wryly.

"Oh . . ." Realizing she'd jumped the gun, she blushed beet red. "Just about."

Hurrying now, she stuffed her damp underwear into the pockets of her jeans—his jeans, that is. If they ran into any of her neighbors along the way, she'd lots rather explain why she was wearing Nick's clothes than why she *wasn't* wearing her bra and panties.

Dovie scrambled to her feet then and took a last look around, trying to see if she'd forgotten anything. "Darn!"

"What's the matter?" Nick spun around, surprised by the vehemence in her voice.

"I dropped my fly rod in the river!"

"That makes us even, then."

"What do you mean?"

The winter wind riveted the icy snow into his face, stinging it, but his smile rippled teasingly, like a summer stream, across his lips. "If that trout's got a lick of sense, it grabbed your fly rod and my sunglasses and headed stright for the Caribbean."

"Your sunglasses!" She whirled toward the river, foolishly bent on jumping in after them, since it was her fault that he'd lost them.

His strong hand shot out to stay her, in a firm grip just above the elbow. "Forget it—they're long gone."

"I'll buy you another pair." Even if it meant a hard-candy Christmas, she'd come up with the money somehow!

"There's an extra pair in the glove compartment of my car." His sinewy fingers squeezed her upper arm in gentle assurance. "My houseman will have them when he comes after me."

Dovie shivered, helpless against the tides of desolation that suddenly swamped her. Oh, dear God, she didn't want him to go!

"You're cold." It wasn't a question; Nick could feel her trembling.

Her teeth had begun to chatter, but it had little to do with the cold.

Without further ado he steered her away from the river, marching her, as if hell-bent, through a barren tangle of wild blackberry brambles and straight up Spicey Hill. The way he moved, sidestepping thorny vines and ducking under snow-laden dogwood and tulip tree limbs, she could hardly believe he was blind.

"Wh—where are we going?" she asked, panting, too rattled even to recognize the path she'd walked alone a million times or more.

Nick didn't miss a beat as he spoke the words that Dovie Brown had never dreamed a man would say to her. "We're going home!"

Three

"I hung your waders in the entryway."

"Thanks."

A fire of pungent cedar and peach wood leaped obediently when Dovie knelt and touched a match to the kindling under the logs she'd laid earlier that morning. "And I stood your fly rod by the front door."

"Fine."

"Sit down and make yourself at home." Rocking back on her heels, she thanked her lucky stars she'd kept that big old fireside chair when she'd divided Pop's things with her brothers and sisters.

"Don't mind if I do," Nick said, and sat.

Not that *she* ever used the chair. With all due apologies to women's lib, it was made for a man, constructed as it was of solid walnut and upholstered in a deep wine leather that wore the patina of paternal love as proudly as it bore the stains and scratches that were inevitable where eight healthy children were involved.

Just seeing how comfortable Nick looked now, his dark head lolling against the tufted back, his tanned hands resting easily on the hobnailed arms, and one bare foot crossed casually over his knee, Dovie felt her heart dance a wild jig of welcome.

The fire grew, its orange-and-crimson light caressing his features as gently as a lover's hand.

From her position on the floor she studied his profile, following the rugged lines of his forehead, nose, and lips, which were lit a burning yellow-red. Scars and all, Nick Monroe was the most attractive man she'd ever laid eyes on.

Enough dawdling, though; she had things to do.

"After I've changed," Dovie said as she stood, "I'll throw our clothes in the dryer and make us some coffee."

"No hurry." Nick sprawled lazily in the cushiony chair, letting the warmth from the fire seep into his bones. In all honesty, he couldn't remember the last time he'd felt this relaxed.

Still, she hovered as nervously as a hummingbird in her bedroom doorway, which opened off the living room. "Maybe I should make the coffee first."

On that note, he sat up straighter and started to stand. "Tell you what: I'll put the coffeepot on while you change clothes."

"But you're—"

Half-sitting, half-standing, he tensed.

"—*company!*"

And the fire punctuated her concern with a pop.

"Why, so I am."

Then the fire breathed a sigh of relief as he bowed to the tradition of Southern hospitality and resumed his seat.

A covey of goose bumps raced up Dovie's arms when he braced his broad shoulders against the leather cushion and stretched out his lean, athletic legs. "I could raise the thermostat if you're chilly."

"Suit yourself," he said smoothly, "but I'll take a fireplace over a furnace any old time."

"Promise you'll stay put?" she asked.

"Where would I go?" He swiveled his head as if looking for the door, then shot a devilish grin in her direction and had the pleasure of hearing her laugh. "You've got my pants."

Her smile wavered as, once again, she hesitated. "Holler if you need anything."

Something in her tentative tone struck a deeply responsive chord in Nick. Having spent the last twelve months learning how to deal with rejection, he could no more refuse her offer than he could climb behind the wheel of his Bronco and drive himself home. "I will."

Dovie left her bedroom door slightly ajar while she rummaged through the drawers in her chiffonier for something to wear. As regularly as clockwork she stuck her head out the opening to make sure she hadn't missed his call.

"Cuckoo!" he teased the third time she checked on him.

Feeling like the biggest fool on two legs, Dovie ducked back into the bedroom and shut the door firmly behind her. Calm, cool, and collected—those were the bywords from here on out! she promised herself. And with that in mind, she took her sweet time about changing clothes.

Nick sat there listening to the sounds that the walls couldn't quite muffle. He heard the rustle of denim and chamois cloth being dropped to the floor. The twang of bedsprings as she sat down to remove his socks. And when all fell quiet again, he pictured a beguiling little vest-pocket Venus in the nude.

Hair and skin so invitingly touchable, it made his fingers tingle . . . opulent breasts that would fill his hands, and then some . . . that wand of a waist, and hips that were nicely rounded but not overdeveloped . . .

Those images, and others, burned holes in Nick's mind as he stared into the darkness at where the door would be if he could see it. *If* he hadn't stopped to help at the scene of that automobile accident that fateful night. *If* he hadn't started back to the tangle of metal and glass to make sure he'd gotten everybody safely out. *If* the damned gasoline tank hadn't exploded in his face.

If, if, if! He clenched his teeth as strongly as he clenched the fist that loudly thumped the chair arm, fighting to keep from sinking back into a black pit of self-pity.

"What was that?" Dovie threw open her bedroom door and peered anxiously around the jamb.

He practically jumped out of his skin. "What was what?"

"I heard a noise, and I thought . . ." Truth was, she'd thought she heard him slam the front door on his way out and she'd panicked.

Ruefully, he relaxed his fist.

For no logical reason, Dovie's skin rippled sweetly when Nick uncurled those long bronze fingers. She looked away, wetting her lips nervously. "Sorry if I disturbed you."

He smelled her attar of roses drifting across the room and lied through his teeth. "You didn't."

"Ah, good." She told herself that her jittery nerves were the natural aftermath of her accident. But she knew that some of her tenseness had to do with standing in her dry bra and panties only a few feet and a partially open door away from Nick. She drew back. "Well—"

"Don't shut the door." He hadn't planned to say that. It'd just popped out.

She was half-dressed; he was all man. Keeping the door open while she finished putting on her clothes would invite a new and potentially hazardous intimacy between them. But closing the door when he'd asked her not to would be tantamount to slamming it in his face.

"I thought maybe we could visit." Suppressed

emotion roughened Nick's voice as he tried to make light of his request. "Besides, it's nothing I haven't seen before."

Sensing the enormity of his need, Dovie acted on impulse. She puffed up her chest, propped her hands on her hips, and adopted a comic Mae West drawl. "I hate to tell you this, Doc, but you ain't seen nothin' yet!"

From the living room came the heartiest laugh she'd ever heard. "Cheeky little broad, aren't you?"

"So I've been told." Warming to the game, she gave her cotton-covered bottom a resounding *whack* with the flat of her hand.

As naturally as night follows day, so compromise flowed from camaraderie. Dovie left the door open but carried her clothes into the half-bath off her bedroom. Nick agreed to speak up loud and clear, something he did almost immediately.

"I like your house." Stiffly starched curtains at the windows and oil-soaped oak floors made it aromatic, while the crackling fire and this comfortable chair he was sitting in made it cozy. All told, he felt a sense of home here—a feeling that had been missing from his life for a long, long time.

"Thanks." She smiled, thinking it was a good thing she'd gone ahead with her annual Christmas cleaning even though she wasn't expecting company for the holidays. "I call it 'the house that hope built.'"

"Why is that?"

"Because Pop built it hoping that three bedrooms would be enough to sleep his family." Dovie slipped on the black scrap-wool pullover she'd knitted during a long rainy spell the past fall. Pushing the sleeves of her sweater back to her elbows she added, "Eight kids later, he finally abandoned hope of keeping up with the birthrate around here."

He gave a low whistle. "Eight?"

"It got so I was afraid to ask, 'What's new?' when I came home from school!"

He laughed. "All grown and gone?"

She paused in the midst of zipping up the matching black pants she'd made on Mama's old treadle-operated sewing machine, a faraway look on her face as she answered, "All gone . . . except for me."

The hint of sadness in her admission hit Nick squarely in the solar plexus. Somehow he knew the answer to his next question even before he asked it. "And your parents?"

"Mama died of childbed fever after Arie, our youngest, was born." She'd forgotten socks. Padding barefoot into the bedroom, Dovie finished telling him about her parents. "Pop died four years later, in a sawmill accident."

"Who raised you kids?"

She swallowed, her heart threatening to explode, her eyes to flood. "I did."

Of course. People from these parts traditionally took care of their own. In the relatively short time he'd known her, Nick had had no reason to think Dovie would do any less.

"And I did a darn good job of it, if I do say so myself!" Tossing her head proudly, she reached into the far corner of her top drawer for that pair of mettalic-gold-and-cardinal-red sport socks that her little sister in Chicago had sent her for Christmas last year.

In the note accompanying the package, Arie had suggested the glitter socks might "jazz up" Dovie's winter wardrobe. Now, looking from her chiffonier to her closet to her reflection in the cheval mirror, she realized she was sick and tired of wearing black or navy blue all the time.

Defiantly she sat down on her bed and drew those gaudy red socks on. Then she stuck her foot out and rotated the ankle this way and that, admiring the look and feel of Arie's gift. Just because a woman was a few birthdays beyond the age of consent, she didn't have to dress like Whistler's mother!

"You're the oldest." Nick stated the obvious.

"Yes." Dovie went on to name her seven brothers and sisters and to brag a little about all their different accomplishments, but he barely listened.

For the first time since he'd lost his eyesight, he was interested in a woman. And not just physically, either, although he freely admitted that her generous curves had him going in circles. No, this was something different. It wasn't merely the flesh he found himself liking about Dovie, but her personality, a staunch spirit in the face of adversity, an ability to take the negatives in life and make them positive.

Nick closed his eyes and clenched both of his hands into fists, cudgeling back a wealth of frustration. The hell of it was, he had nothing to offer a woman anymore. Especially one who'd already seen her share of sorrow. So where did that leave him? Ready to cut his losses and run, that's where!

"If you're hungry," she offered as she came out of the bedroom, "I could make us some hash."

His whole body went still. The hunger he felt had nothing whatsoever to do with food. "That's not necessary."

"Have you eaten?" Dovie crept cautiously across the living room toward the laundry room, trying not to fall on her recently waxed floor. Her boots weren't dry yet, and her new red socks were slippery on the bottom.

"No." As though to remind him that the trout breakfast he'd planned on hadn't worked out, Nick's stomach growled. "But don't go to any trouble on my account."

"Oh, it's no trouble." She threw their wet clothes in the dryer and set the timer for an hour, then made her way on cat's feet to her small Shaker sewing rocker, opposite Nick's chair. Funny, how she suddenly considered it *his* chair. "Really! I always cook enough to feed an army—habit, I suppose— and you're more than welcome to join me."

"Homemade hash?" His deep tone sounded so

wistful that Dovie couldn't help but smile. "With potatoes and onions and a poached egg on top?"

"Is there any other kind?" she teased as she lowered herself into the rocker with a heartfelt sigh of relief.

He remembered all those canned goods lining his kitchen shelves back at the cabin and the remaining vestiges of his reluctance vanished. "Well, if you're sure you don't mind—"

"Pish tosh." Sitting and chatting with him in front of the fire like this, she felt a momentary pang for what might have been had she chosen to marry. "I'd love the company."

"And I'd love a decent meal for a change," he confessed with a disarming smile. "Harley is a terrific driver but a terrible cook."

"Harley?"

"My houseman."

"Oh, right."

Nick stood at the same that that her Seth Thomas mantel clock chimed half-past eight. "Which reminds me, I'd better give him a call and tell him about the change in plans. He was going to pick me up on the river road at nine."

"The telephone's in the kitchen." Dovie saw him stiffen defensively and realized her mistake.

Ignoring her first instinct, which was to take his arm and lead him across the room, she sat perfectly still and added, "Turn right and take about"—she studied the muscular length of his legs, trying to calculate—"five steps. It's a wall phone. You can't miss it."

"Wanna bet?" he grumbled good-naturedly. By following her directions to the letter, though, he did find the telephone.

"We're in a different area code than Richmond." Naturally she assumed he wanted to call his home there.

"It's a local call." He met the truth head-on as he reached for the receiver. "I've rented a cabin about a half mile west of where we were fishing this morning."

She looked at him, stunned. "You lied to me about where you live?"

"I didn't lie." He dropped his hand. "I really do live in Richmond."

"Silence can be a lie."

He knew she was right. He'd deceived her by his silence, hoping to keep her at arm's length. But in the long run he'd outsmarted himself. He took a hard breath. "What can I say? I was—"

The telephone rang, cutting him off in mid-sentence. As though it were the most natural thing in the world, Nick answered it. "Hello."

"Who's this?" the caller asked point-blank.

Rudeness begat rudeness as Nick replied in kind. "Who wants to know?"

"Curtis Lee Brown, that's who!" His booming declaration carried clear across the room.

At that, Dovie catapulted from her rocker and

fairly skidded across the highly polished floor in her stockinged feet.

"Now, who the hell are you," her brother all but bellowed, "and what are you doing in my sister's house at eight damn thirty in the morning?"

"Maybe you'd better explain it to him," Nick said, handing her the receiver.

"Dovie Ann, are you all right?" Curtis demanded.

"Of course I'm all right." Anger ripped through her voice as she released some of her pent-up pain on her brother. "And where do you get off calling up here and lighting into my guest like that?"

"I was just surprised, that's all," he admitted, then added tactlessly, "I mean, it's not every day a man answers your telephone."

Honestly, she thought, she wanted to reach through the telephone wire and strangle him! "It's not every day I fall in the river, either."

"What?"

Both the sting of Nick's rejection and the shock of his deception began to fade as Dovie described her fall and the way his quick action had saved her life. She left nothing out. Quite literally he'd given her a second chance. In return she gave credit where credit was due.

Nick lazed back against the wall, feeling guilty as sin as he listened to Dovie praising him to the skies. He'd badly misjudged her and he owed her an apology—no two ways about it. But he wasn't good at making apologies. Never had been, and probably never would be.

Her intense tone suddenly piqued his professional interest. "Did you call your doctor? Do you need to borrow my car to drive her to the hospital? . . . What does he mean, it sounds like flu? How can he sit in an office fifty miles away and tell flu from labor?"

Dovie drew in a deep, calming breath then. "Well, it's not going to do either one of us any good to get mad, but it's at times like this that I wish the plans for our clinic hadn't fallen through. . . . Tell you what. Come get my car and take Linda into Richmond so the doctor can examine her properly."

On the other end of the line, Curtis lowered his voice to a confidential level.

"Right," she replied softly.

While Dovie waited for her brother to relay her message to his wife, she directed her attention to Nick. "Curtis said to tell you he's sorry he yelled at you a moment ago, but with no doctor nearby and his first baby showing signs of being born two weeks early, he's just about reached the end of his rope."

"No hard feelings." Nick shrugged nonchalantly, thinking he could certainly tell her a thing or two about hanging on by a thread. Against his better jugement he asked, "How far apart are your sister-in-law's pains?"

"They're not really pains per se," Dovie admitted reluctantly. "Curtis said she woke up shivering, with a splitting headache, and now she's complaining of mild stomach cramps."

Obeying an impulse that was overwhelming for all that it remained nameless, Nick pressed on. "Is she spotting? Has her water broken yet?"

"No. But when Mama went into labor with our twins, Merle and Mary, she had symptoms similar to Linda's." Dovie put her hand over the mouthpiece, Nick's sudden interest sparking an idea. "If Linda were *your* patient, what would you suggest she do?"

"She's not my patient!" he rebuked her rawly, shoving himself away from the wall to stand with his back to her, his head bent while he rubbed his neck. "And don't ask me to second-guess her physician!"

Shocked and hurt by his outburst, she stared at him. "You initiated this conversation, Nick, not I."

"Damn!" He cursed the darkness that engulfed him, hating it more with each passing day. Still, he didn't come right out and say he was sorry. "I didn't mean to snap at you, Dovie, but—" He bit off his sentence and turned to face her, grim lines bracketing his sensuous mouth. His shoulders were tense, braced against the terrible impact of his memories. "It's just that obstetrics was my favorite part of practicing family medicine—the light at the end of the tunnel, so to speak."

He smiled, but Dovie realized it was merely a polite movement of his lips rather than an expression of humor. "As hokey as it sounds, I used to hold those small, squalling, squirming bundles of joy in my arms and think, 'Maybe this one will discover the cure for cancer. Maybe this one will become President someday. Maybe this one will bring a lasting peace to the earth.' "

Tears filled her eyes as she noted the way Nick's strong, sure hands sliced the air for emphasis. Law, she felt the loss as deeply as he did! Struggling for control, she cleared her throat. But before she could speak, her brother came back on the line.

"Linda says she's feeling a little better now that I've turned up the thermostat and she's had something warm to drink." Curtis seemed a lot calmer. "She also says she doesn't want to ride to Richmond in a snowstorm, then have to turn around and come home again, if it's nothing more serious than the flu."

"Well, don't let it go on *too* long," Dovie admonished. The memory of her mother's untimely death haunted her.

"Dr. Rodgers is right on top of this." Curtis voiced complete confidence in their family physician. "He's always on call, even through the night, and I promised to notify him if there's the least little change in her condition."

"Joe Rodgers?" Nick asked when he heard the name.

"Yes." Without so much as a second thought, Dovie turned to him for reassurance. "Do you know him?"

"We interned together. And if it relieves your mind any, I'd trust him with my life."

"It does." She perked up immediately. "Thanks."

"Say what?" her brother asked.

"Here, ask him yourself." Dovie handed the receiver to Nick so he could talk to Curtis, then went to put the coffeepot on.

Nick shook his head as he hung up the phone. "Is it always this hectic around here?"

"Not so much now that the kids are gone." She removed a foil-covered package of leftover corned beef from the refrigerator. "But there're still times I meet myself coming and going and wonder where I've been—especially when my nieces and nephews are here."

He laughed and reached for the receiver again. "I hope I haven't missed Harley."

Dovie wanted to ask him why he hadn't told her right off the bat about the cabin he'd rented, but she was afraid to rock the boat. He was entitled to his privacy. And he certainly didn't owe her any explanations.

But if it was privacy he was seeking, she thought as she took a skillet from the drawer at the bottom of her stove, he'd come to the wrong place. Spicey Hill was home to the nicest, *nosiest* bunch of people she'd ever heard had existed on this planet. And she'd bet dollars to doughnuts, once word got out that there was a doctor in residence, even briefly, he'd be swamped with calls.

"Harley said the roads were getting slick, so I told him I'd meet him down by the river at ten-thirty." Nick snapped the thread of her reverie with his report. After washing his hands at the sink, he asked her expectantly, "Is there anything I can do to help?"

She clamped her metal food mill to the edge of the counter top and began grinding chunks of corned beef onto a piece of waxed paper she'd spread. "You can set the table when it's time to eat."

"Fair enough." He went to the stove and tested the heat of the burner by waving his hand over it. "Coffee's done."

"Here, I'll pour us some." She crossed to the hard-pine hutch where she kept the blue-marble enamelware that Mama had set up housekeeping with and got two cups.

"*I'll* pour," he insisted.

And to Dovie's everlasting amazement, Nick did exactly that—filling the cups he'd taken from her without spilling a drop.

"I listen for the liquid to reach the right level and then I stop," he explained, correctly surmising that she was dying of curiosity. Turning, he held out her cup. "Cream or sugar?"

"Will wonders never cease?" Her fingers brushed his when she took the cup, and she stood like a statue feeling the touch of a magic wand, suddenly imbued with life-giving current.

"I hope not." Something good was happening to him, *had* been happening to him all morning. He was laughing again. Arguing again. Caring again. It was like opening an old wound that hadn't

healed properly and pouring antiseptic on it. Ago-
nizing as hell. But worth it, if one could look
beyond the pain.

Nick smiled, flowing with the feelings, and
unerringly clinked his cup gently against hers in a
toast. "To wonders. May they never cease."

"I'll drink to that," Dovie said, and did.

Outside her clapboard house, a banshee wind
howled and the snow tittered its secrets against
the windows. Inside, steaming black coffee and a
budding attraction warmed two strangers through
and through.

"Would you mind fetching me an onion from the
pantry?" Dovie peeled and diced a couple of cold
cooked potatoes she'd found in the crisper. "It's
the first door to your left," she added automatically. "The onions are hanging in a braid on a hook
to your right."

Nick brought back the whole shooting match,
because he had no idea in hell how to remove one
onion. "Did I smell pumpkin and dried apples in
there?"

"Sure did." She cut an onion off the bottom of
the braid, peeled and minced it, and dropped the
pieces into the frying pan to brown in a teaspoon of
bacon drippings. "Thanks to my garden, my hogs,
and the occasional trout, I rarely have to shop for
groceries. In fact my only cash income is from this
farm; the hogs provide most of my money."

"You raise hogs?" If she had suggested they go

skinny-dipping right after breakfast, he couldn't have been more amazed.

"Prize blue guineas," she boasted.

"Isn't that dangerous?"

"No. Why?"

"Because hogs bite."

"Only under duress." Lifting the onions from the frying pan with a slotted spoon, she mixed them with the corned beef and potatoes in a blue wooden bowl. "Anyway, I've got the most laid-back hogs this side of the Mason-Dixon line."

"You're so little, though," he argued. "What would you do if one of them attacked you?"

"Wave a white flag?"

"Be serious, will you?" His stentorian tone told her he was taking this very seriously.

"Look," she said, then sighed. "I know you're concerned about me. And I appreciate it—I really do. But with Christmas right around the corner and my sister-in-law ready to deliver at the drop of a hat, being attacked by a hog is the least of my worries."

Dovie shaped the corned-beef mixture into patties and arranged them in the oil sizzling in the skillet. "Besides, blue guineas aren't that big and I'm not all that little, although it's certainly nice of you to say so."

What in the sam scratch got into Nick he couldn't say, but the next thing he knew, he'd taken two steps backward and cocked his head to the side as though he were sizing her up. "How tall are you, anyway?"

"Five foot none," she answered saucily.

A crooked grin tugged at the corners of his mouth. "Cute."

"Don't ever call a short person *cute*."

"Why not?"

"Because she just might haul off and punch you in the knee!"

He laughed openly, throwing his head back and thinking how much he would miss her lively banter when he left. "And begging your pardon beforehand, what do you weigh?"

"A hundred and plenty." Her hourglass body tended to be a touch hippy; she wouldn't have divulged that information under penalty of death!

"Five foot none and a hundred and plenty, huh?" A sly smile limned his lips. "Sounds like a bite-sized snack for a stressed-out hog."

And then they were both laughing, when it wasn't really *that* funny, and she took her turn thinking she sure would miss this man's wonderful sense of the ridiculous when he went home.

She sobered at the reminder and reached for a pan to poach their eggs in. No sense brooding about something she couldn't change. "Breakfast is almost ready, so you can set the table now. Salt and pepper are on the stove; butter's in the icebox."

Like most doctors, Nick was better at giving orders than he was at taking them. But without a word of argument he set their two places cozily at right angles on her dining-room table, arranging the napkins and silverware and condiments so he wouldn't have to grope for them.

While she waited for the water to boil, Dovie watched the smooth play of his shoulder muscles beneath his thermal shirt. Finally realizing what she was doing, she spun away and plopped two pieces of rye bread in the toaster. They popped up just as she'd finished filling their plates, and she joined him at the table.

For all their talking and teasing beforehand, they ate in silence, their appetites duly reflecting the fact that their metabolisms had been running full tilt all morning.

"That was good!" Nick exclaimed. He sat back and let out a repleted sigh. "If you fed your brothers and sisters that well, I'm surprised they ever left home."

Dovie started to pick up their empty plates, thought better of it, and sat back too. The dishes could wait. It wasn't as though she had anything else to do later on. "I'm afraid home cooking runs a poor second to matters of health."

He arched a thick black eyebrow quizzically. "What's that supposed to mean?"

"It means if we had decent medical facilities here on the hill, more of our young people—my brothers and sisters, for example—might stay and raise their families."

"That's right; you said something about plans

for a clinic falling through, when you were talking to Curtis."

"He'll leave next," she said mournfully. "I just know it."

"Maybe not." But something told Nick that was small comfort.

"He's already talking about it." Dovie reached for her coffee cup, saw it was empty, and dropped her hand. "Linda's had a difficult pregnancy, and they've about worn themselves sick running to and from Richmond to see the doctor. Then, to top it all off, the brakes on their ten-year-old Chevy went bad and the auto-parts store is closed through Christmas, so they have to borrow my car when there's an emergency."

Nick shook his head in sympathy. "It sounds like Curtis can't win for losing."

"That's not the half of it!" Too agitated to sit still any longer, Dovie stood and began clearing the table. "If Curtis and Linda leave, can my other brothers—Jack and Ray and Lon—and their familes be far behind?"

He rose to help her. Their hands collided in midair when they both reached for the butter dish. She drew her breath in sharply, and his actions stilled for a heartbeat. Then she pulled her hand away as though she'd just been burned, and he picked up the cut-glass dish. Perversely, he was glad he wasn't the only one who felt such a soul-jolting thrill whenever they touched.

She stood stock-still, captivated by the sight of

his hand, with its long fingers curled around the fragile dish, the dark hairs swooping down from his forearm and wrist as he set it on the counter. At the thought of that hand on her body the blood thundered in her ears, echoing through her head until she thought it would surely burst.

The timer on her dryer buzzed, and in the furthest reaches of her mind Dovie feared the worst had happened, that her head really had burst. Then she realized what it was and made a sound like air going out of a balloon. "Oh, good . . . our clothes . . ."

"Can't wait to get rid of me, huh?"

She looked at him to find that teasing smile back on his lips, and said softly, "You're welcome to stay for the day, as far as I'm concerned."

He sobered and crossed to her mantel, silently counting his steps, then opened the hinged face of her clock and felt the hands. "It's almost ten; I don't want to miss Harley."

"Fine." She swallowed hard, drowning a hope she hadn't bidden, and clapped the dishes she was carrying into the sink. "I'll get your clothes."

His spicy citrus scent, fresh as the outdoors, clung to his warm chamois-cloth shirt. The legs of their jeans, his so much longer than hers, had tangled into a veritable lover's knot during the drying cycle.

She separated them with a wistful smile, squared her small shoulders, and took his clothes to him. He was dressed and ready to leave before she could say Jack Robinson. She trailed him to the door, her heart suddenly heavy as lead.

"I'd be happy to drive you down to the river road," she offered when he reached for his waders.

"No, thanks." Nick felt her eyes boring into his back and half turned, towering over her in the small entryway. "I need to learn my way around."

"Oh, of course," Dovie agreed too quickly, and backed a step away from him, only to trip over his fly rod, which still stood by the front door.

He reached for her wrist to keep her from falling. "Are you all right?"

"Yes," she whispered miserably, knowing that he must think her totally graceless, a real klutz.

A smile softened his strong jaw when she was finally steady on her feet. She was so fragile, as delicate as china. He released her reluctantly and leaned down to pick up his fly rod. "Listen, thanks for breakfast."

"My pleasure." Anxiety made her voice breathless.

He turned and opened the door. "Good-bye, Dovie."

She shivered and hugged her arms against a cold chunk of despair. "Good-bye, Nick."

Halfway out the door he stopped and weighed his decision for a few seconds before turning back. "Will you meet me at the river tomorrow?"

"T-tomorrow?" she stammered, so startled by his abrupt about-face that she could hardly think.

"If you'd rather not—"

"No . . . I mean, *yes*, I'd like that very much."

"Same time?"

The snow swirled in about her feet, blanketing those garish red-and-gold socks in winter white, but summer blossomed in her smile. "Same time."

"See you then," he confirmed before closing the door softly behind him. And for the first time since he'd lost his eyesight, Nick was looking forward to tomorrow.

Four

A good six inches of snow lay on the ground the next morning and a pale gray sky presaged several inches more before nightfall, but nothing short of an avalanche could have deterred Dovie. Clutching tightly the split-bamboo rod and graphite reel that had belonged to her father, she practically slalomed down Spicey Hill.

Slightly winded, as much from the excitement of seeing Nick again as from her race against time, she paused at the bottom to catch her breath. Inhaling deeply . . . exhaling slowly . . . She finally felt her pulse return to normal. She shouldn't have bothered. The instant she spotted him, her heart went bobsledding again.

He'd claimed her favorite spot, of course, but had cleared a place to his right for her. Sharp-combed waves chopped at the rocky bank where he stood with feet spread wide and fly rod at the ready, his rugged masculinity harmonizing perfectly with the wild river setting.

Moving with the precision and power of a mountain cat stalking its prey, he made a perfect cast. His lure arced high in the air, catching a bitter angling breeze that carried it twenty feet or so before it landed with a soft *plop* and sank.

Upstream a flash of silver suddenly caught her eye.

Then another.

And yet another.

Incredible as it seemed—especially on the first cast—he'd flushed a school of trout feeding in a small chute of water between the rocks.

Dovie had been so absorbed in watching Nick that she hadn't moved; she was still a dozen yards behind him. But now, her fishing fever soaring to an all-time high, she ran to the riverbank and rigged up. With any luck she'd catch her Christmas dinner this morning!

"You're late." He said it solemnly, but his warm smile bid her welcome. The opaque sunglasses that hid his eyes were identical to the ones he'd lost yesterday.

"Appears to me I'm just in time," she replied sassily as an enormous trout circled, white-mouthed, around his lure.

Nick wanted to tell her that truer words were never spoken. That he'd been a dead man inside before her musical laughter and womanly body had brought him back to life. He wanted to say he was sorry he'd made her mad yesterday morning . . . sorrier still that he hadn't kissed her. But knowing it was too much too soon he said, "You certainly are," and let it go at that.

The trout seized both his lure and his attention then, snapping cold spray in his face as it turned abruptly and sped for shallow water. He slammed the bail of his reel open and let the line sing free in spiraling loops so it wouldn't break, then clinked the bail shut and began working his rod.

Dovie stood in utter awe of Nick's strength. Last night she'd lain awake in her lonely bed, thirty-four years old and fast heading upward, and found herself wondering if perhaps she'd endowed him with powers he really didn't have because she craved some excitement in her life. But the moment she saw his lithe muscles rippling beneath his hunter's-plaid shirt, she knew he was everything she'd remembered . . . and more.

"Oh, hell!"

His words pierced the still, frosty air, startling her. She looked closer and saw that the trout had run up under a rock and tangled his line. He reached to clear it, his pliant fingers expertly plucking the eight-pound test.

The trout darted into deeper water, fighting him ferociously, and Dovie could hear the stressed fiberglass strands in Nick's rod humming like high-tension wires.

She couldn't begin to guess how long the fight

lasted. It might have been five minutes, or fifteen. She only knew that her arms ached for him as he strained against losing the fish. That her legs grew heavy and her breath came hard while he stoically stood his ground. And that her knees went rubbery with relief when he finally brought the trout home.

"Hand me the net, will you?" Nick reached out behind him, and she rushed to do his bidding.

"It's beautiful," Dovie murmured after he'd scooped up his second big rainbow in as many days.

The trout had nearly torn the hook free, and it slipped out easily.

"The next best thing to breakfast at Tiffany's," he stated with justifiable pride. His fingers were numb from the fight and the freezing water, but when he cradled his prize with both hands he felt a pang of shame.

For reasons she couldn't define, Dovie sensed his change of heart. "You're not keeping it."

"I can't."

"Why not?"

Nick held the trout upright. "Feel her sides."

"*Her* sides?" But as she ran her hands along those bulging flanks, she suddenly understood that the deep and eternal force of life was trying to repeat itself in the trout's body. "She's ready to spawn."

"Her eggs are so ripe, she's about to explode."

And Dovie, who'd once decided against marrying

and having children because she'd raised so many relations, now felt her own biological clock ticking like a time bomb and wondered if she'd made the right decision. "No wonder she fought you tooth and nail; you threatened her babies."

The trout gasped, her gills heaving harshly.

"Come on, little mother, I'm taking you home." Nick crouched and swam the trout into the current, wagging her tail back and forth until she'd revived sufficiently to hold her place in his loosely cupped hands.

Dovie watched from the bank as he retraced the path of their fight in stages, holding the trout behind each rock in turn and letting her adjust to the swifter currents before moving her on.

When the trout was strong enough to swim, she slapped her tail against Nick's arm as if to say thank you, then shot out of his hands. Dovie saw her for an instant in that wintry water, a speedy silver-gray missile. And then she was gone.

He turned toward the bank and grinned. "Oatmeal, anyone?"

She laughed softly, still pondering the import of what she'd witnessed and its impact on her. "Would you settle for sausage and cornmeal mush?"

Cocking his head and hooking both thumbs in the waistband of his waders, he pretended to give that serious consideration. "I might."

Like metal shavings to a magnet, Dovie's eyes were drawn to the opaque sunglasses he wore. She pictured his deep blue eyes, crinkled at the corners in amusement beneath coal black brows, and wished she could see them again. Her voice drifted wistfully across the water. "I'll even throw in a pot of coffee and let you pour."

Nick's laughter flowed as richly and warmly as the blackstrap molasses she was planning to serve with breakfast. "You drive a hard bargain, lady, but I sure do like your style."

She watched him climb the bank, taking it slowly but surely, and wondered if he would kiss her this time. The thought sent chills chasing along her spine and spawned an earthy sensation somewhere below her stomach. Only when he pushed his sunglasses back onto his head did she know for certain that he would.

His nostrils flaring slightly as he inhaled her heady rose fragrance, Nick homed in on her. Her pulse racing ecstatically at the hard-muscled sight of him, Dovie dropped her fishing rod and moved into his embrace as naturally as if she'd known him for years.

Yesterday he'd told her she was beautiful; today he showed her how beautiful she really was.

Holding her as though she were fragile and precious, Nick lowered his face toward hers. His lips trailed fiery paths across her cheeks, her eyelids, her chin, burning away the December chill.

Dovie trembled feverishly in his arms, but he didn't rush. He paid homage to each perfect feature, that delicate bone structure; he even took the time to savor the honeyed flavor of her breath.

Every sense she had woke up and sang. She felt the imprint of his hard body against her softer one. Inhaled deeply of his lime-and-spice soap. Heard him fashion her name in low staccato sounds that echoed her heartbeat. And when his mouth finally met hers, the taste of him went straight to her head.

Intoxicating he was, like Christmas Day brandy, and she parted her lips to drain the cup.

Suddenly, so suddenly she almost lost her balance, Nick thrust her from him and turned away. In the sorry shadows cast by the naked trees, his breath tore out in ragged white clouds. "Dammit, Dovie, if I don't stop now, I won't be able to."

Touching trembling fingers to lips still deliciously damp from him, she swallowed the bitter pill of his rejection and forced herself to speak calmly. "That's funny; I thought I gave you the green light."

His harsh laugh ripped a big hole in her heart. And a bleak wind whistled through the opening when he flipped his sunglasses back in place and turned on her. "In case you haven't noticed, I'm color-blind!"

"Well, if you're looking for sympathy, you can find it in the dictionary." Dovie's voice shook dangerously as anger flooded in to fill passion's void.

"I'm not." Nick's tone held all the warmth of surgical steel. "But if I were, you can damned well bet you'd be the last one I'd look to."

"Thank God for small favors," she snapped. Then, stricken by guilt at what she'd just said, she spun away from him, her rubber waders slicking in the snow. Through all the years, all the crises . . . no one and nothing had ever rattled her as much as Nick just had!

"Listen"—he sighed heavily and reached for her arm, trying to make amends—"that remark I made about being color-blind was a real cop-out."

From the corner of her eye she saw his hand coming at her, and stepped sideways to evade it. "Yes, it was."

"And I really can't believe that I was stupid enough to let a good thing end so badly." He grabbed a fistful of freezing air and ground his teeth in frustration. Then he lashed out with his left hand.

Dovie's conscience warred with her pride as she dodged him again. She wasn't playing fair, of course, but she'd be hanged for a horse thief before she'd stand still for any more of his abuse! "Me either."

"About the only excuse I can offer is that shortly after I was blinded, I was surrounded by women who thought I needed them to 'take care' of me." Remembering all the nameless, faceless bodies he'd bedded during those first dark months, Nick stopped and raked an aggravated hand through his thick black hair. "I suppose they saw themselves as sexual therapists or something, and I—"

"If you think I'm interested in hearing you brag

about how many notches you've carved in Braille on your bedpost, you're sadly mistaken!" she snapped over her shoulder.

"You jump to conclusions faster than a frog!" Veering toward the sound of her voice, he grabbed her arms in a steel vise of a grip and jerked her around to face him. "Now, you're not making another move until I've had my say! Understand?"

Dovie stood frozen in his grasp, stunned by the anger that had erupted in him. Dimly she realized that he wasn't angry at her as much as he was angry at the terrible fate that had robbed him of his eyesight. Nevertheless, Nick in a temper was a man to fear.

"I don't blame you for thinking I was bragging a moment ago, but believe me, I wasn't." He relaxed his grip but didn't release her, because he was sure she'd bolt if given the chance. "And I know you were mad when I stopped kissing you—"

"I wasn't mad; I was hurt."

Nick could feel her trembling through the nubby cotton fabric of her sweater. The way his knuckles were still digging into the sides of her breasts, he knew her courage must have cost her dearly. "I never meant to hurt you."

Dovie heard the change in his voice, but it did nothing to calm the riotous vibrations where his hands held her captive. Her fear of him was gone, replaced by a fear of a different kind. A fear of herself. "Then let me go."

Silently, he did as she had demanded.

It was almost full daylight now. Around them snow fell softly from laden evergreen boughs and icicles on the nearby dogwood limbs began to melt under the fleeting magic of a December sun. Between them their breaths joined in warm white clouds on the freezing air. And together they braved a whole new world of emotion.

"I don't know about you," he said huskily, "but I'm a hell of a lot friendlier on a full stomach."

"Me too." Giving in to an impulse she'd had since she first met him, she raised one hand and let her fingers sift through his windblown hair. Ah, it felt as clean and springy as it looked.

"The offer's still open, then?" He caught her hand and brought it to his mouth, pressing his lips into the center of her palm with a light, experienced touch that made her ache with excitement deep inside.

Dovie nodded, illogically thinking he could see the motion.

Nick sensed it and, giving in to some devilish impulse of his own, murmured against her sensitized skin. "Then let's go home. I'm starved."

"Oh . . . you . . ." She let out a huff of laughter and snatched her hand away. "Just for that, you have to make the coffee as well as pour it."

He laughed too. "Sounds good to me."

They gathered up their fishing gear in companionable silence and started back. As they climbed the hill, their footsteps crunching through the snow, she was suddenly acutely aware of winter's beauty.

"Be my eyes," Nick said, placing a proprietary hand at the small of her back. "Describe everything you see, starting with the sky."

Dovie searched the sky as desperately as she scrambled for adjectives. They had to be absolutely perfect. "Polished pewter."

"Polished pewter?" A twist of a smile touched his lips, and she felt foolish for having gotten so carried away by a gray sky. Then her tension receded and relief flowed in when he laughed triumphantly. "Beautiful! Clear as a bell!"

After that, it was a snap.

"What's the snow look like?"

"Diamond dust."

"The trees?"

"Straight out of a Currier and Ives Christmas scene."

A pair of cardinals whistling in the pines . . . chirring chipmunks playing tag under the drooping canopy of a willow . . . a white-tailed doe and her spotted fawn poised for flight halfway up the hill . . .

The snowscape was so beautiful that Dovie wept because Nick couldn't see it. At the top of the hill she stood next to him, his arm around her shoulders. He touched his hand to her face, where he found her tears.

"It's that lovely, is it?"

She nodded, knowing he felt her response, and laid her cheek against his warm, wide chest.

The sharp air lashed at his face, and his lungs filled with it, clean and crisp. Winter held the world in its icy fingers, but Nick held Dovie, and something hard and cold within him began to thaw.

"No one's ever cried for me before." He bent his head and kissed away her tears, his mouth so tender, she thought she might swoon. "Thank you for being my eyes."

"I should be thanking you." Listening to the strong, steady beat of his heart, she sighed contentedly, a kind of peace stealing over her. "I've been so preoccupied lately, I'd almost forgotten how pretty it is around here."

They stood in silent communion with each other and with their own emotions for a while longer.

For Dovie, who'd given up her youthful dreams to take care of her seven brothers and sisters, it was a chance to dream again. And for Nick, who had taken a little over a year to come to terms with the loss of his sight, it finally was time to look to the future.

What neither of them realized in the dawn of a new day was that this was simply the calm before the storm.

After ten rings, Dovie hung up the telephone receiver, sighed, and turned back to the stove.

"Still no answer?" Nick had paused in the midst

of setting the table, his head tilted at a listening angle. The instinct born of years of medical experience, of being aware that what patients didn't say was often more important than what they did say, had alerted him to Dovie's distress.

"No." The word was softly spoken, emotionless, but he knew anxiety too well to miss it in someone else. She was worried sick because she couldn't locate Curtis and Linda.

"Try the hospital again," he suggested.

"I've already left messages with the admitting office and the maternity ward," she said.

Dovie felt a cloak of guilt closing around her. Even though her brothers and sisters were on their own, they still depended on her in case of an emergency. And rightfully so. Remembering the way she'd snapped at Curtis when he'd called her yesterday morning, she blinked back tears of remorse and set about finishing the cooking of their breakfast.

The pungent aroma of sage and coriander trailed her to the table when she carried in a platter of hot homemade sausage patties. Napkins and silverware were unnecessarily rearranged right under Nick's nose. A friendly, crackling fire received several unfriendly thrusts from the tip of an iron poker, provoking a snapping shower of sparks in return.

Killing time . . . Nick knew damn good and well what Dovie was doing. Massacring the moments until she could go back to the telephone and try her brother's number again. And all the while she was keeping that tightly controlled silence that people who've never had anyone to share their burdens with are prone to keep.

For all intents and purposes she'd forgotten he even existed. So he waited patiently while she plumped sofa pillows and straightened family photographs with a mother hen's practiced hand. And he wondered, as she busyworked her way back to the table, how many times she'd walked these floors alone, the worries she'd inherited weighing heavy on her mind.

Compassion and the need to help her welled up strongly in Nick. He was deluged by the desire to hold her and calm her. To protect her and to provide the missing years of love and laughter that could never be made up for.

"I'll get the mush," she finally said.

"Forget the mush."

"But I've got to call—"

"Don't shut me out, Dovie." He reached out and grabbed her wrist, gathering her into the comforting circle of his arms.

"No!" She resisted him fiercely at first, twisting and turning, drumming his chest with her frantic little fists. "Let . . . me . . . go!"

But he needed her as much as she needed him, so he clasped her to him all the more closely until, like a broken spring, she unwound suddenly and burrowed into his arms.

"Hold me, Nick, hold me, hold me, hold me."

"I'm here." He bent his head and buried his face in the soft clean silk of her hair.

Her breath was warm and labored on his neck. "I'm afraid."

"A fear shared is a fear conquered."

That seemed to do the trick. Her body sagged with relief and her breathing returned to normal. The fingers that had clutched handfuls of his shirtfront with such desperation began to relax.

For a long time neither spoke. Dovie slid her arms around his lean waist and let herself rest against the hard bulk of his body. Nick registered the crush of her soft breasts against his chest, the shape of himself against her stomach, but kept his thoughts to the straight and narrow. The embrace was one of sustenance rather than desire, a drawing of strength, and perhaps a prelude to tragedy.

"Something's happened to Curtis and Linda," she said at last. "I can't explain it, but I can feel it in my bones."

Dovie had never given birth; her brothers and sisters had grown in her heart, not under it. In raising them, though, she had developed that age-old intuition that is part and parcel of motherhood. And it was her maternal sense of urgency to which Nick responded.

"I'll put the food away while you back the car out."

"There's a shortcut through the woods," she said, "but we'll have to walk."

"Fine." He turned her toward the table. "We'd better hurry."

They had the food put away and were out the door in a matter of minutes. Snow fell needle-straight now from churlish clouds that seemed to make dusk of day. In the distance a lone dog howled its misery, while the wind moaned about something that hurt. The morning had lost its luster, which only added to Dovie's dread. But even if worse came to worst, she would never forget how safe and protected she'd felt in Nick's arms.

It was beginning to look at lot like Christmas at Curtis and Linda's. A boxwood wreath adorned with chinaberries and lemons hung on the front door. On either side, brass-and-glass carriage lanterns wore ribbons of red. A willow basket full of apples—symbolizing generosity and goodwill—had been left out on the wooden step.

Outside, their small saltbox home extended a warm holiday welcome to one and all; inside, it was as cold and silent as a tomb.

Five

"Where's their bedroom?" Nick demanded after a quick but thorough search of the basement and first floor proved futile.

"Upstairs." Dovie's stomach went weightless with alarm when she looked past the fragrant pine swags that looped their way up the banister. Why, oh, why, hadn't she called them before she left to go fishing this morning?

Fear dampened her palms and dried her throat as she hurried toward the stairs. "Here, I'll show you."

"No!" Nick's fingers curled around her arm, stopping her short of the first riser. He knew she was already torturing herself needlessly, and wanted to spare her as much as he could. "I'll go."

She rounded on him. "But—"

"But nothing!" The doctor within him, for a time

69

imprisoned in some dark part of his mind, was back in control. "You call Harley and tell him to bring my medical bag. He knows where I keep it. And tell him to alert Joe Rodgers . . . just in case we have to take them to Richmond."

For a moment Dovie felt as if she might be sick. Then she swallowed, willing herself to take strength from Nick, to trust his decision, and finally she nodded. "What's your telephone number?"

He gave it to her and then bounded up the stairs, using the greenery-decorated banister as his guide.

"Five steps down the hall, first door to your right!" she called up just as he reached the second-floor landing. Then she ran to the telephone and dialed his number with shaking fingers.

"Curtis?" Nick paused outside their closed door and laid his ear against the wood, listening. "Linda?"

When no one answered—had he really expected otherwise?—he found the doorknob and turned it. Flinching slightly because of the cold, he entered the eerily silent room.

Luckily the bed was only a few steps from the door. He leaned down to explore it and felt them curled spoon-fashion beneath the covers, as though trying to share their body heat.

Working rapidly now, Nick rolled Curtis onto his back, pressed two fingers just below his jaw, and made out a thready pulse. Then he moved to the opposite side of their big four-poster bed and repeated the procedure on Linda, with the same results.

"They're alive." He answered Dovie's unspoken question when he heard her hesitate in the doorway.

"Thank God," she murmured. Her anxious gaze lit on the taut swell of Linda's stomach. "What about the baby?"

Nick threw back the quilted bedspread along with a host of blankets, lifted the hem of Linda's flannel nightgown, and pressed his fingers against the lower left quadrant of her protruding abdomen, feeling for the fetal heartbeat.

Watching . . . waiting . . . Dovie bit her bottom lip so hard, she drew blood.

Suddenly Linda's stomach began arching and changing shape, as if her baby were waking from a long winter's nap.

The instant she saw the infant move and realized what it meant, Dovie almost wept with relief. But this was neither the time nor the place for tears, so she stepped to the bed and asked with brisk intensity, "What do you want me to do?"

Nick palpated Linda's distended abdomen with both hands, the shadow of a smile tingeing his lips when he located the baby's head in the birth canal. If everything went as it should . . . Abruptly he pulled the hem of her nightgown down, snapped erect, and ordered, "Close the door and open the windows."

"Right." But the room seemed to spin as Dovie rushed to do his bidding.

The window closest to the bed slid up smoothly, but the latch on the storm was stuck.

She tried working it loose, becoming all thumbs and butterfingers in the process. Then she rested for a moment, her thoughts suddenly muddled, while thousands of tiny pinpoint lights exploded in front of her eyes and the world reeled around her.

Finally, sensing that time was of the essence, she mustered every ounce of strength left in her and tried the latch again.

It gave.

Dovie pushed up the thermal pane, then dropped to her knees. Cold air swirled in, clearing her head. The snow that had piled up against the storm window collapsed and fell onto the bedroom floor.

Not until Nick knelt beside her and drew in several drafts of the fresh, freezing air did she understand what an incredibly close call they'd just had.

"How do they heat this house?"

"Curtis converted from oil to gas a couple of years ago." She looked at him quizzically. "Why?"

"Unless I've missed my guess, their furnace has a carbon-monoxide leak."

"But the pilot light was on when we checked the basement."

Nick stood, and Dovie followed suit. "A lit gas burner only means the furnace is operating; it has no bearing on the CO."

She opened the rest of the windows without a hitch, and the room immediately felt like the inside of a meat locker. "CO?"

"The odorless, colorless, silent killer." He scooped Linda up off the bed and carried her to an open window for some fresh air.

"I never even suspected it." Dovie shivered, not entirely from the cold, when she sat down on the window seat and helped Nick lower Linda to her lap. Later she would remember with amazement how they had worked as a team. But the danger was still too recent. Still too real. "Law, we could have died—all of us!"

"That's my fault." He briefly relived another reaction, the one that had cost him his eyesight. Surprisingly enough, the memory wasn't nearly as bitter now as it had been a couple of days ago. Before he'd met Dovie. Dear Lord, if anything had happened to her because of him . . . He crossed back to the bed, appalled at his own recklessness. "I didn't stop to think that carbon monoxide can put the rescuers at risk too."

Watching Nick heft her two-hundred-pound-plus brother with no more difficulty than he'd have picking up an infant, Dovie felt a surge of emotion that ultimately clouded her eyes. "When will they start coming around?"

"The sooner the better." His thigh brushed hers when he sat down next to her and turned sideways so Curtis could get a lungful of life-giving air. The strength of his physical response to touching

Dovie really jolted him, and it was all he could do to check the urge that stiffened his jeans.

"Are you saying they still might . . . ?" Fear made sailor's knots in Dovie's throat, and her voice faded to nothingness.

Nick reached over with his free hand and squeezed her shoulder, wishing he could absorb some of her pain. His heart thundered when he felt Dovie's first soundless spasm, the sob that was not yet a sob. She was so alone . . . so vulnerable.

Deep in her own misery, Dovie rubbed her palms over Linda's abdomen. As she did it she felt the muscles begin to tighten, starting at the sides and rippling upward. Suddenly she felt immensely relieved, then full of excitement.

"Look, Nick!" She took his hand and laid it at the base of her sister-in-law's stomach, then placed her own on the opposite side.

Their fingertips touched, their hands forming a light cradle around Linda's abdomen as, together, they shared the thrilling affirmation of life amidst the tragic possibility of death.

"She's in labor, isn't she?"

"The first stage of it, yes."

"Did you hear that, Linda?" Dovie spoke excitedly into her sister-in-law's ear. "The *doctor* says you're in labor!"

Nick didn't have the heart to correct her.

When a tiny foot—or was it a fist?—poked at the flat of her palm, she leaned over and shook her brother's shoulder. "Your baby kicked me, Curtis!

Here"—she took his limp hand and held it in place—"feel for yourself!"

Linda shifted restlessly then, as though she recognized her husband's touch, and Nick felt a little chill that had nothing to do with the cold air flailing through the bedroom when his burden, too, began to stir.

"Where the hell is Harley?" Rationally he knew it had only been about ten minutes since Dovie had called his houseman, but it seemed like hours.

Her gaze skimmed the empty road in front of the house, then swung to Nick. He held his head in an alert pose, his profile a bronze relief carving in the sepia light of winter. Until now, she'd been too preoccupied to notice that he'd removed his sunglasses. "He said he'd be here as soon as humanly possible."

The unspoken question hovered between them: But would he be in time?

"High forceps."

Dovie stood quietly in a secluded corner of the delivery room, every nerve, muscle, and sense strained to the limit as Dr. Rodgers prepared to take Linda's baby. This was the moment of truth, what the battle in the bedroom and that hair-raising ride with Harley had been all about, and her eyes automatically sought Nick's reassuring presence.

Like everyone else in the room, herself included,

he wore baggy surgical greens. A loosely-tied cap hid his thick black hair, while a gauzy white mask covered his crooked nose and mobile mouth. He stood to the right of Dr. Rodgers, his head cocked at that vigilant angle she'd come to associate exclusively with him. Dovie thought it must be a trick of the bright overhead lights that made him seem to shimmer and vibrate with new energy as the crisis neared conclusion. But something told her he was simply back in his element.

She couldn't see very well from where she stood, but she didn't dare voice a complaint. A high-forceps delivery was an exceedingly difficult and dangerous operation, indicated now because the baby was too far into the birth canal for a cesarean section. Dr. Rodgers had been adamantly opposed to her presence during the procedure. Only after Nick intervened on her behalf, citing her experience as midwife for her mother, had the reluctant physician relented.

Linda lay draped and anesthetized on the delivery table, her eyes closed peacefully and her chest rising and falling to the rhythm of the ventilator. She'd been told the truth when she'd asked, that Curtis was alive but too weak to be with her, and Dovie could only pray that her sister-in-law somehow sensed that she wasn't totally alone in her time of travail.

"Blood pressure," Dr. Rodgers demanded.

"One-thirty over eighty," the nurse-anesthetist answered.

Thinking that sounded a little high, Dovie looked at Nick. He seemed to realize she was worried and nodded reassuringly.

"Forceps," Dr. Rodgers ordered.

"Forceps," the scrub nurse repeated before placing it in his gloved palm with a firm snap.

If she lived to be a hundred, Dovie would never forget the almost palpable tension that gripped the room when Dr. Rodgers went after Linda's baby. She trained her gaze on Nick, reading in his body language what she couldn't see.

When sweat beaded on his brow, perspiration rolled in rivulets down her stomach and thighs. If he listened to the fetal monitor overly long, her pulse did a three-minute mile. And when he leaned over and reached out, her heart flew into her throat.

"It's a boy," Dr. Rodgers announced.

Nick straightened up, laid the blue-gray baby on his mother's belly, and gently massaged him. "Start the oxygen and get his blood gases."

"Yes, Doctor."

Dovie could hardly breathe as she watched her new little nephew. His head was covered with wet, downy black hair, almost like a fledgling bird. When Nick rubbed his back, he opened his mouth and gave a mew. Before her eyes, he began to bleach and pinken. Ribs tiny as a sparrow's sprang outward—she could see their whiteness through the skin.

Suddenly he screwed up his face and screamed,

shaking a fist wildly at the great surgical light. That cry carried the wattage of chain lightning, burning away the tension and bringing thanks to the hearts and lips of all who heard.

Dr. Rodgers looked up from between Linda's swaddled knees, admiration and relief evident in his eyes. "It's good to know you've still got that magic touch, Dr. Monroe."

It might have been Dovie's imagination, but did Nick nod in *her* direction? "That remains to be seen, Dr. Rodgers."

The coffee in the doctors' lounge was the consistency of crankcase oil, but it could have been smoothly blended whiskey, for all that Nick had noticed. He crumpled his empty Styrofoam cup, dropped it in the wastebasket, and headed for the door. "Catch you later, Joe."

"Hey, wait a minute!" Joe Rodgers grabbed his stethoscope and hurried into the hospital corridor after him. "I'm going that way, too, so we might as well walk together."

"Oh?"

"She went to tell her brother about the baby."

Nick nodded and turned in the direction of the Intensive Care Unit, where Dovie was.

"Fine figure of a woman."

"And a damned nice one, too."

"It's about time."

Nick chuckled softly. "If that's a polite comment

on all my one-night stands after the accident, I couldn't agree with you more."

"Polite, hell!" Joe laughed out loud. "For a while we had a running bet around here on which you'd need first—a Wassermann test or a rabies shot."

Nick grimaced in self-disgust. "Hell, don't remind me."

"Perfectly natural reaction, punishing yourself like that after such a significant loss."

"Thanks, Sigmund," Nick said dryly.

"You're *v*elcome," Joe replied, deadpan.

They both laughed.

"So . . . how'd you meet her?"

"Trout fishing." Remembering how he'd pulled Dovie out of the river, Nick smiled. But Joe's next remark brought him up short.

"Still trying to drown your sorrows, huh?"

"It sure beats making brooms," he retorted bitterly.

"How does it compare to the thrill of holding that new life in your hands this afternoon?"

Nick clenched his teeth. "It doesn't, and you damn well know it."

"Or the satisfaction of hearing that woman say thank you when you diagnosed her diabetes simply by smelling the fruity aroma on her breath several years back?"

"What's the point of rehashing the past?" he asked scoffingly, more disturbed then he cared to admit.

"The point is, you still have a place—a future, if

you will—in medicine, but you're the only one who can find it."

At the entrance to the Intensive Care Unit, Joe exerted a gentle guiding pressure on his elbow. "First door to your right. I'll be in as soon as I check the latest lab report on her brother's blood gases."

Nick's senses were instantly heightened. The blipping monitors . . . the antiseptic odors that seared his nose and throat . . . the very urgency of the air. Damn, but it was almost a drunken high!

Thirsty for more, he stood in the hallway for a moment, pondering Joe's insightful comment. Suppose . . . just suppose he actually hung out his shingle again. A bitter curl lifted one corner of his lip. What patient in his right mind would consult a blind doctor?

Dovie's delightful laughter floated from the cubicle where her brother lay recovering from his near-fatal bout with CO intoxication. At the door Nick paused and reached into his shirt pocket for his sunglasses. Remembering that he'd left them on the nightstand in Curtis and Linda's bedroom, he swore softly under his breath.

"Nick—" The name came so naturally to her lips! "I mean, Dr. Monroe." Confused by her own confusion, Dovie linked her arm through his and drew him toward the bed. "I'd like you to meet my brother."

After the introductions were made, Curtis mumbled unintelligibly.

"I *think* he said thank you," Dovie said, her breath catching in her throat for a second when her breast brushed against his muscular arm. "He can't talk with the oxygen mask on, so I'm serving as his interpreter."

Her brother's eyes, however, spoke quite eloquently, narrowing with angry disapproval when she continued to cling to Nick. Embarrassed without knowing why, Dovie let go of his arm.

But when she started to move away, he laid a staying hand on her slender waist, the warm pressure of his fingers seemingly burning through the fabric of her sweater as he held her possessively at his side.

She looked up and was startled to see that his jaw had gone as hard as teakwood. The machine monitoring her brother's vital signs began blipping a little faster. She glanced at Curtis. What was visible of his face behind the oxygen mask was as red as ribbon candy.

"Oh, Curtis, I can't wait till you see that baby. He's a doll! And Nick, you'll never believe how much he looks like Curtis did when he was born. A carbon copy!" She realized she was rambling to hide her nervousness.

Nick sensed it, too, and replied simply, "We'd better go now so Curtis can get some rest. He's had a pretty rough time of it today."

Her brother's face turned fuchsia.

"I know, but . . ." Law, why did she feel so torn between family loyalty and her own desire to be alone with Nick? She'd paid her dues. Hadn't she? "Shouldn't we wait to hear what Dr. Rodgers has to say about his lab tests?"

A host of perceptions hit Nick all at once. From the monitor, which was running a little rapidly but still well within normal limits, to Dovie's sudden reluctance to leave, it was obvious that Curtis was trying to lay a guilt trip on her. And doing a damned good job of it, too, judging by the dismay that laced her tone.

"All right." But just so Curtis would know that *he* knew what was going on, Nick retained his possessive hold on Dovie.

"You're a lucky young man," Dr. Rodgers said to Curtis when he stepped into the Intensive Care cubicle. "The tests show that the level of carbon monoxide in your blood has almost returned to normal. But if it hadn't been for Dovie and Dr. Monroe, your people would be planning a burial instead of a baptism."

"How's Linda?" Dovie asked anxiously.

"She's fine. Her anesthetic during the delivery was ninety-five percent oxygen. We've moved her from the recovery room to the maternity ward, if you'd like to stop and see her before you leave."

"And the baby?"

"Beautiful." Joe Rodgers clapped Nick on the shoulder and grinned from ear to ear. "Every baby is a miracle, of course, but when *this* baby screamed while you were massaging him, I got goose bumps."

"I'll have to admit to a little nervous chill myself." Nick's hand trembled slightly as his thumb moved upward and lightly stroked the side of Dovie's breast.

Like electricity his touch jolted her every cell. She stood rooted, suddenly not knowing how to act or what to say. At last she turned to Dr. Rodgers. "What caused the carbon-monoxide leak?"

"Purely speculating now, I'd have to say a clogged furnace vent." He glanced at Nick. "I seem to recall your treating a case very similar to this one several years ago, so what do you think?"

Nick nodded. "That would be my guess too. See, over a period of time, the soot that's been deposited on the chimney liner during the oil-burning process is loosened by the greater amounts of condensed water vapor produced by the new gas system. Eventually, clumps of soot fall, blocking the vent."

While Nick went on to warn that everyone who converts a furnace from oil to gas should have the chimney cleaned, he settled his hand just under Dovie's breast.

She didn't look at Curtis for fear of the censure she'd find in his eyes. No man had ever laid a hand on her in front of family. But neither did she say or do anything that could be construed as an objection to Nick's familiarity. No man had ever made her feel this much a woman.

Dr. Rodgers turned to Curtis. "I'll probably release you tomorrow, so I'd suggest you make arrangements to have your chimney cleaned before you move back in."

"It's already been taken care of," Nick said. "Harley and a man from the gas-service company went back to their house while we were in the delivery room."

By the time Dovie bid Curtis good-bye, his monitor was going like mad. It gave her a twinge of guilt, but, after telling herself he was in the best possible hands and promising him that she'd check on Linda and the baby, she left the Intensive Care Unit without a backward glance.

"Dr. Rodgers." A disembodied voice paged him through the hospital corridors. "Dr. Rodgers, please report to Surgery."

"A doctor's work is never done." He smiled at Dovie and shook hands with Nick. "I'll see you two on Saturday night."

Then he turned and headed down the hall.

"What did he mean, he'll see us on Saturday night?" she asked as they waited for the elevator that would take them up to the maternity ward.

"Joe and his wife, Elaine, are giving a Christmas party for the hospital staff, and"—a surprising vulnerability entered his voice—"he asked me to bring you."

Once inside the elevator, she broke the bad news. "I'd love to go, Nick, I really would, but I always baby-sit for my brother Jack and his wife, Jayrene, on Saturday night."

He cornered her—literally and figuratively. "Well, you'll just have to tell Jack and Jayrene that the man who saved your life wants to collect his reward."

Caught between his powerful body and the wall, Dovie felt totally defenseless. "But they're counting on me."

"So am I."

She looked up sharply. "They need me."

Nick leaned down and let his tongue do the talking. The silken tip of it skimmed her bottom lip, bathing it with his own nectar. Then it traced her top lip, all sleek, wet satin . . . and oh, so tempting. When she opened her mouth to welcome him home he murmured, "So do I."

"Please . . ." Reeling, she reached out and sought the support of the waist-high railing that branched out on both sides of her.

"Twenty years you've given your brothers and sisters." Moist lips moved over hers with gentle sipping motions, and her slumbering senses awakened with an intense craving to experience everything she had missed. "Your high-school prom and your graduation party. College and the career of your choice." Gifted hands conformed her supple hips to his hard heat. "Marriage and a family of your own."

"Please . . ." Dovie felt her nipples budding and her body flowering open, preparing for love. How many Saturday nights had she tucked someone else's children into bed and wished to be doing something else? Something like this. Flustered, she wrenched her mouth away. "Please don't ask me to choose. Not again. Not so soon."

"Twenty years," Nick repeated thoughtfully as his long, blessed fingers lovingly feathered the back of her neck. "It's not everyone who'd do that, Dovie, especially in today's world. Do you regret it now?"

"I . . ." Stricken, she realized she didn't know how to reply. When the elevator doors whooshed open, she pushed past him and dashed out.

But there was no escaping the truth. It followed her into Linda's room, where her sister-in-law radiated a serenity that Dovie envied to the core of her soul. It stalked her to the nursery window, where she stood with her fingertips against the glass and tears glistening in her eyes. The fact that she hadn't denied her regret was the closest she'd ever come to admitting it.

"Does it help to know that I think you did a hell of a good job raising your brothers and sisters?" Nick stood behind her, not touching her, just there in case she needed a shoulder to cry on.

"Yes." A sob escaped her throat when her new little nephew opened his rosebud of a mouth and set up a great big howl. "But what I regret more than anything is the way I used them to excuse my own inadequacies."

"How so?" he prompted softly.

"Do you want to know *why* I missed my high-school prom?"

"Only if you want to tell me."

"It wasn't because I couldn't afford a baby-sitter, which is what I told people and which was easier to deal with than the truth." She dropped all pretense of dignity and began to cry in earnest. "It . . . it was because no—nobody invited me."

Nick turned her toward him and gathered her gently into his arms. Dovie cried against him with her elbows folded tightly between them, and her tears brought some new and disturbing stinging behind his eyes. When her sobbing eased, he took her face in both hands and wiped at the wetness on her cheeks with his thumbs.

"Do you want to hear something else?" She hiccuped indelicately and laid her head against his chest. "I've known for a couple of years that it was time to cut the apron strings and get on with my life. Last winter, when I learned about a grant program that trains nurse-practitioners to give primary care in rural areas like Spicey Hill, I even went so far as to send for an application."

"Did you submit it?"

She shook her head, and a lock of her soft, clean hair tickled his chin. "No. I was so afraid that I'd be accepted and then found wanting, I threw it away."

Running scared . . . Well, he could certainly relate to that. Hell, he'd been running at Mach

Four ever since that gasoline tank had exploded in his face.

She worked her arms out from between their bodies and slipped them around his lean waist. "It's kind of funny, really. At the time, I told myself that the kids still needed me too much. But when you asked if I had any regrets, I suddenly realized that I was the one who was all tangled up in the apron strings."

"I've got a nice sharp pair of scissors in my medical bag." Nick crushed her closer and they clung that way, sharing a new bond of warmth and comfort. "I'd be glad to cut you loose, if you'd like."

"I'd like." Her voice was so low, it vibrated. "Do you know what *else* I'd like?"

"Food, I hope." His stomach grumbled noisily. "Sorry, but it's a well-known fact that man does not live by excitement alone."

She gave a gasp of surprised laughter. "Law, this must be one for the record books! I haven't thought about food in almost twelve hours."

"Well, put your thinking cap back on, because I'm buying dinner."

"Now that you've mentioned it, I'm starved!"

He released her and grinned. "What was it you wanted to say before I so rudely interrupted you?"

Dovie turned to look again at her newborn nephew, as pink and round and perfect as a Christmas angel. The confusion and weariness of the day, the worries and sorrows of a lifetime, fell away from her like a worn-out robe.

When she finally turned back to Nick, she felt the fluttering of hope in her heart. "I wanted to say that if the invitation for Saturday night is still open, I'd like to try my wings."

Six

Cupping the telephone receiver between her shoulder and her ear, Dovie reached around behind her back and zipped up her new dress. "No kidding, Arie, when I looked in the mirror after that man was through with me, I said 'This isn't a makeover. It's a miracle!' "

Her youngest sister's laughter caroled merrily over their long-distance connection. "Well, it's about time you spent some money on yourself."

"It wasn't that expensive, if you want to know the truth." Perching on the edge of the bed, Dovie slipped her slender feet into black satin pumps. "All they charged me for was having my hair styled. They did my makeup for free—some sort of a sales promotion. But I'll probably be a month of Sundays paying off the clothes I bought to complement the new me."

"What color is your dress?"

"Would you believe fire-engine red?"

Arie whistled appreciatively. "I'll bet it's smashing with your dark hair and doe eyes."

Smashing? Dovie stood and examined her reflection in the cheval mirror across the room. It was the most daring dress she'd ever owned!

The crushed-silk halter top lifted and supported her generous breasts, while leaving her shoulders and back seductively bare. Soft torso shirring and the long, pencil-slim skirt accented her other hourglass attributes. Her only jewelry was a new pair of jet eardrops, but her sequined cardigan sweater was guaranteed to light up the night.

Standing in front of the mirror in the boutique, her confidence buoyed by a two-hour session with the beauty consultant, she had thought she looked pretty glamorous. But now, seeing the woman in red reflected in her own mirror, she feared she'd gone too far in trying to make a silk purse out of a sow's ear.

"How's Linda?" Arie asked.

"Oh, she's fine." Stretching the telephone cord as far as it would go, Dovie began rummaging frantically through her closet for a different dress to wear tonight. "I stopped by the hospital before I went for my make-over this morning, and she said the doctor is going to release her tomorrow."

"Who does the baby look like?"

"A clone of Curtis." Glancing back at her bedside clock, Dovie saw that she had less than an hour to undo the damage before Nick picked her up for the party. She grabbed the first thing she found, a simple wool crepe sheath—in black, of course—then turned and took a bra and slip out of her chiffonier drawer.

"I'll bet Curtis is just busting his buttons over that baby."

"I suppose." Remembering the way he'd snubbed her when she entered Linda's hospital room earlier that day, Dovie felt angry and guilty at the same time. It was ridiculous! He was behaving like a spoiled brat and she was wondering where she'd failed him. She sighed and reached around behind her back again to unzip her beautiful red dress.

"What's the matter?"

"What do you mean?"

"Come on, you can't kid an old kidder. Something's wrong and I'm not hanging up until you tell me what it is."

The line grew silent for a long time, with only some distant electronic beep making noises in their ears. Dovie gripped the phone with both professionally manicured hands. She desperately needed a sounding board, but she'd never dreamed it would be her little sister.

She finally exploded. "You're right; something *is* wrong! It's the abominable way everyone in this family is acting now that I've started seeing Nick."

"Everyone?"

Dovie never knew before that she could hear a smile. "Except you, of course."

"Go on, I'm listening."

"Well, Curtis hasn't given me the time of day since I left him in the Intensive Care Unit. You'd think I'd abandoned him, when, in reality, he and Linda and the baby wouldn't even be alive if Nick and I hadn't rushed over there that morning. And Jack's been in a snit ever since I told him I couldn't baby-sit because I was going to a party tonight. Then yesterday, both Lon *and* Ray had the gall to call me up and tell me I was behaving like a teenager!"

Dovie paused then and drew a deep breath. "Whew! Who've I left out?"

"Mary and Merle."

"Oh, right. How could I have forgotten Mary's reaction? When she stopped by this afternoon with a dress she wanted me to hem, she took one look at my hair and makeup and burst into tears."

"You haven't gone punk, have you?"

"Of course not." Dovie looked closely at her reflection in the mirror. The hair at her crown had been layered to release its natural body, while the sides were smoothed behind her ears with a little styling mousse to highlight her facial features. The makeup had been done tastefully, giving her cheeks delicate hollows, her eyes luminosity and depth, and her lips a bead of light as if she'd just wet them with her tongue. "Quite frankly, I like the new me!"

"Last but not least, there's Merle."

"Oh, you know Merle . . . he thinks 'Thou Shalt

Preserve the Status Quo' is the Eleventh Commandment."

"That may be part of the problem."

"Come again?"

"Did you ever stop to think that the 'old them' might need some time to adjust to the 'new you'?"

She hadn't, of course. Dovie mulled that over while she zipped up her red dress and hung the black one back in the closet. "I guess people grow at different rates, don't they?"

"Right. Even though you're changing for the better, you have to remember that we're a fairly conservative family, for the most part, and prepare yourself to wait it out."

"That could be a long siege."

"Maybe; maybe not." Arie's shrug was almost audible. "The other thing you have to remember is that when you change, people have to change the way they react to you. For instance, they can't assume you're going to baby-sit on Saturday nights; they have to ask."

"Which they should have been doing all along," Dovie added a little peevishly.

"Yes." Arie's pause was eloquent. "But you've always let them assume you were available, so—"

"So I wear a share of the blame."

"If the shoe fits . . ."

"Perfectly." Dovie glanced down at her new black pumps and smiled as realization dawned.

"See, even a small change in your physical appearance, such as wearing makeup, when you've never worn it before, forces people to look at you in a different light. And if they aren't ready to do that, it can cause some resentment on their part."

"Hm, you may be right."

"I know I'm right," Arie said with emphasis. "Take it from me, enrolling in the Art Institute of Chicago was the smartest move I ever made. It not only offered me the opportunity to develop my artistic talent; it also gave me a chance to be treated as an adult rather than the baby of the family."

As she'd confessed to Nick the other day, Dovie had been plagued by a similar sense of dissatisfaction for a couple of years now. Only her own fear of failure had prevented her from acting on it. "Are you saying that I should leave home too?"

"Not necessarily. I know how much you love Spicey Hill. But if you stay, and if Curtis and Jack and the rest of them continue to behave the way they have been, you'll have to confront them sooner or later."

"What I'd really like to do is turn each and every one of them over my knee!" Dovie burst out.

"It's no less than they deserve," Arie agreed. "But since they all outweigh you by at least thirty pounds—Mary included—you'll probably have to be satisfied with a tongue-lashing."

The line buzzed voicelessly for a few seconds before Dovie laughed. "How did you get so smart at the tender age of twenty?"

"I had a good teacher . . . and the most wonderful surrogate mother in the whole world."

"Would you settle for best big sister? Surrogate mother makes me sound older than Spicey Hill."

"Consider it settled."

They chatted a while longer, mutually lamenting the fact that Arie's part-time salary as a window dresser for Marshall Field's wouldn't stretch far enough to include both a trip home for the holidays and next semester's tuition at the Art Institute.

Before they said good-bye, Dovie mentioned that she was giving serious consideration to submitting an application for the nurse-practitioner's program, and Arie expressed wholehearted approval.

"You've certainly got the compassion and the common sense it takes to be a good nurse."

"Talk about your late bloomers, though. I just realized I could be the oldest living college freshman."

"Better late than never. The most important thing is that you never stop growing and never stop enjoying. Besides, nobody tells a rose when to bloom."

Dovie cleared her throat. "Thanks. I needed to hear something like that."

Arie laughed. "Listen, I'd better go before I have to make a choice between paying my tuition or my telephone bill."

"I'll call you Christmas morning," Dovie promised. "I'll be here alone, because everyone else is staying home to start their own traditions, so we can talk to our hearts' content."

The line went quiet again. After a long time Arie said, "I just hope Prince Charming knows how lucky he is."

"To tell you the truth, I'm pretty lucky myself."

"I love you."

"I love you too."

Only after they hung up did Dovie realize that she'd never told Arie that Nick was blind.

"Merry Christmas," Nick said when Dovie opened the door half an hour later. It might have been a trick of the moonlight, but his deep blue eyes seemed to hold a mischievous sparkle.

"Merry Christmas," she answered, smiling a small, nervous smile as soon as she saw he was wearing a black cashmere topcoat that had obviously been tailored to accommodate his broad shoulders.

The blood leaped wildly to her face when he held a sprig of mistletoe over her head and leaned down to kiss her. He simply touched his mouth to hers, but even that brief contact had her brain short-circuiting.

"Do you want to try for Happy New Year?" Nick asked teasingly.

"Happy New Year," she echoed softly.

At that, his tongue breached her lips to flirt with

the tip of hers, and Dovie could feel the titillating caress all the way down to her toes.

"What next?" he asked.

"Groundhog Day?" she offered.

Laughter bubbled between their lips as he tossed the sprig of mistletoe over his shoulder and opened both his arms and topcoat to give her a brief glimpse of a black tuxedo that, combined with a snowy wing-collared shirt, gleaming onyx studs, and a silk bow tie and cummerbund, made him look like a walking ad for *Gentlemen's Quarterly.* "What the hell, Happy Groundhog Day!"

A symphony of rustling silk and rapid breathing, Dovie lost herself in warm cashmere and hot-blooded male. Nick's tongue took its natural course, making exquisite love to her mouth, while his hands massaged her bare back with equally sure strokes. Strangling in delight, she molded her hips to the source of his wonderful heat and answered his message with trembling lips.

"If that's Groundhog Day," she whispered when they finally drew apart, "I can hardly wait for the Fourth of July."

"Fireworks," Nick promised, pulling away from her reluctantly. "Now, go get your coat and car keys before I turn into a Roman candle right in front of your big brown eyes."

Dovie handed him her spangly new sweater with a stab of apprehension. Maybe she'd mistaken flashy for formal! She stood with her back to him, scarcely able to breathe, while he slipped it over her shoulders.

"Sequins?" He ran his hands down her arms, fingering the small flat disks as intently as if he were reading Braille.

"Yes," she admitted miserably, wishing now she'd done the sensible thing and worn the black wool crepe.

He toyed with her sequin-encrusted cuff, trying to complete his mental picture. "What color?"

Thinking she might as well get this over with, Dovie repeated the description she'd given Arie a little earlier. "Fire-engine red."

Everything clicked with perfect clarity in his mind's eye. Laughing triumphantly, Nick touched his lips to the side of her neck. "I love it!"

"*Really?*" She'd been so certain that he would hate it, his enthusiasm caught her completely off-guard.

"Really." He heard the relief in her voice and realized just how much she valued his opinion. "It's beautiful. And besides"—his smile expanded on his words—"where else am I going to find a woman who makes me see red?"

"Oh, you . . ." Spinning around, she punched him lightly on the arm. But her merriment filled the entryway as surely as it filled the long-empty hollows of his heart.

"Where's your coat?"

"I'm wearing it."

"That's a sweater, not a coat," Nick argued. "And it's only fifteen degrees above zero outside."

"So I'll think warm," Dovie said dismissively.

He remembered the way he'd found her in the river, wearing nothing but her bra and shirt, and the truth hit him with the force of a blow.

She didn't have a coat.

Instead of pressing the issue—or embarrassing her by offering her his coat—Nick simply put his arm around her shoulder and tucked her against his cashmere-clad body as they walked out to her car.

"I'm not cold," Dovie protested. But it felt so good to know he cared, she didn't pull away.

"Your metabolism must operate in overdrive."

"I credit the cold baths for it."

He opened the door on the driver's side and thought of roses in the snow when he caught a whiff of the pleasant scent threading from her. Only after he'd buckled himself into the passenger seat did he ask, "Cold baths?"

"Pop swore by them—the colder the better." She kicked off her satin pumps, fearing she'd catch a high heel in the hole she'd worn in the carpet, then put a nylon-encased foot on the accelerator, and started the engine. "He believed they kept a person healthy."

"In other words, he was practicing preventive medicine?"

"With eight children and no doctor nearby, what else could he do?"

Nick draped his arm across the back of the seat, not touching her, yet making her heart careen when she realized how close his hand hung to her breast. "Exactly what he did, I suppose."

"Right." The road was so slick, Dovie shifted into low and drove slowly downhill. "Every Saturday night he'd line us up in the hallway according to age—yours truly in front. Then he'd say, 'Think warm,' and have us take turns in a bathtub of icy water."

For the first time he thought he understood why she had such an upbeat attitude. "It sounds like your father used a little psychology on you, too."

"Psychology?" At the bottom of the hill she pulled out onto the highway. The sound of the tires told her it had recently been sanded.

"The whole time he was toughening you up physically, he was also teaching you the power of positive thinking."

"I never realized that before, but it must've worked, because we're the most disgustingly healthy family that ever walked the face of the earth."

Nick let his hand drift to the side of her neck and allowed himself the luxury of stroking that smooth, slender column while he said teasingly, "*And* the most accident-prone."

"I'll have to admit we've had our share of emergencies lately." Dovie kept her eyes on the road, but every nerve in her body began dancing to the tune those clever fingers were playing on her skin.

"Am I bothering you?" he asked when he felt her pulse accelerate.

"A little," she admitted breathlessly.

"Should I move my hand?" He started to do so.

She shook her head, and he put it back where it belonged. "By the way, did Harley like that tin of Christmas goodies I sent home with you the other day?"

"The bourbon balls were fantastic."

"Maybe I should rephrase my question." Dovie laughed. "Did Harley *receive* that tin of Christmas goodies I sent home with you the other day?"

"We shared them that same night. He loved the peanut brittle, but it played havoc with his false teeth." The tip of Nick's middle finger drew lazy circles on the tingling flesh of her nape. "You got your hair cut."

"Styled," she corrected throatily.

"Cut, styled, whatever, I like it."

"You do?"

"Sure. Why? Don't you?"

"Yes, but . . ." A shudder rippled through her when his thumb traced the sequined neckline of her sweater.

"But you thought men preferred women with long hair?" Sensitive fingers felt her nod. "Now, I ask you, what man in his right mind would prefer long hair to this lovely neck?"

His words touched her in a way his hands and kisses had not, deep within. She struggled for a reply, then settled for a simple and sincere, "Thank you."

They rode in silence, Nick's hand bridging the distance between them, until they reached the city limits. Then cool air replaced his warm palm on her neck. And through the back of her thighs Dovie felt his weight shift on the car seat as he removed his sunglasses from his coat pocket and put them on. Maybe it was only her imagination, but it seemed to her that he used them like a mask.

Following his directions, she turned right and headed down Monument Avenue. Lined with towering statues of General Lee and other Southern heroes, bordered by skeletal trees strung with white lights, and fine old houses in various stages of restoration, the broad boulevard had touches of sorrow, pride, and dignity, all at once.

"I hope you know where we're going, because I sure don't," she said as they entered a neighborhood of elegant, snow-swept lawns that bespoke estates rather than lots.

"Have I ever steered you wrong?" he asked teasingly.

"There's always a first time." She followed the curving street until she found the cobblestoned driveway he'd warned her to watch for.

Nick unbuckled his seat belt and turned sideways, his nostrils almost flaring because of the light rose fragrance emanating from her. "Well, what do you think?"

Dovie couldn't control a soft gasp of delight as

they rolled to a stop in front of the beautiful red brick house sitting atop a gentle hill. "Law, it looks like a miniature Monticello!"

The windows were all ablaze, throwing oblique patches of golden light across the snow of early evening. Each of the four columns supporting the second-floor balcony wore twining streamers of greenery studded with small red bows, while a large wreath trimmed with rubrum lilies, clusters of Christmas balls, and tiny wrapped gifts decorated the front door. A liveried attendant stepped off the portico, as though anxious to hand the lady from her coach-and-four.

Shiny Cadillacs and sleek Mercedeses lined the drive. As the attendant rounded the rusting bumper of her ancient station wagon, Dovie panicked. "There are so many fancy cars here that maybe I should let you out and go park around the corner."

Nick laughed and leaned down to retrieve her shoes from the floor. "No way."

Visions of melted nylons danced in her head as incendiary fingers captured her ankle and fevered hands replaced her black satin pumps. When her car door swung open, she could have sworn she heard violins.

"Come on, Cinderella." Nick fairly waltzed her through the moonlit night and into another world. "They're playing our song."

* * *

The middle-aged physician smiled and delivered the punch line. "So *I* said, 'Socialized medicine is when the doctor takes his clothes off too!' "

Dovie looked around with studied casualness, then slowly backed away from the laughing crowd. Nobody seemed to miss her, which wasn't the least bit surprising, but still—

She accidentally bumped into a couple making a fast turn around the dance floor. Her glass fell from her hand, and Dovie watched in speechless horror as the white wine she'd been nursing for the last half hour spread down the front of her new dress.

The couple came to a dismayed halt. The man murmured helpless apologies, but the woman grabbed the handkerchief from her partner's pocket and started mopping the stain.

"Such a shame," the woman said sympathetically.

"I'm sorry; I wasn't watching where I was going." Feeling miserable, Dovie caught sight of Nick across the room. He stood near the buffet table with a remarkably beautiful blonde, whose lustrous hair cascaded down to the middle of her back. Tall and slender and looking like some expensive Christmas ornament in a chic creation of pale lavender shot with silver, she was everything Dovie was not.

She was also one of a half-dozen women—maybe more—who seemed to have decided that Nick needed them to take care of him. All evening these beautiful women with their perfect figures and designer clothes had cleverly elbowed Dovie aside to feed him, lead him, mother him in cool, elegant ways. When the blonde raised a forkful of caviar-stuffed potato to his firm lips, Dovie's spirits plunged so low that she seemed to hear them hit the ground with a thud.

"Maybe if you went to the bathroom and put some water on it . . ." the woman she'd bumped into suggested.

"Yes, thank you; I'll try that." She turned her back on Nick and the blonde, but the picture rankled until something pinched her throat and made it difficult to speak. After dabbing at the silk with water, she went in search of a place to dry out.

Dovie stood in the library door. If the rest of the Rodgerses' house suggested hospitality on the grandest scale, this room breathed privilege the likes of which she'd never known. There were thousands of books here, packed tightly on shelf after shelf, holding much of the wisdom and storied charm of the ages.

Enchanted, she approached a book-lined wall as reverently as one approaches an altar. The wonderful smell of leather bindings might even have been incense. Awed fingers touched titles stamped in gold. Humbled eyes scanned works ranging from one end of the literary scope to the other.

A voracious reader who wasn't above perusing the backs of cereal boxes when money for books was in short supply, Dovie felt sure she'd died and gone to heaven.

Impetuously she kicked off the black satin pumps that had her hobbling like Chester in "Gunsmoke" reruns and took *Gray's Anatomy* from the shelf. Then she curled up in one of the chairs facing the hearth.

She was so deeply absorbed in the medical book that she almost jumped out of her skin when, about half an hour later, Nick called her name. Embarrassed by her skittish reaction, she closed the book on one index finger and sat up straighter. "What?"

"I said I've been looking high and low for you." He crossed the library with the confident grace of a frequent, welcome guest.

"Oh." Dovie watched him come toward her. He was so tall and strong and perfectly groomed, and she was suddenly, painfully conscious of her damp dress and bare feet. She put the book back on the shelf and began scrounging around for her shoes.

Nick heard her crawling around on the carpet and stopped so he wouldn't step on her hand. "Would you mind telling me what the hell you're doing down there?"

"Looking for my shoes."

"Of course," he muttered wryly. When she stood, the strength of her "eau de Chablis" nearly knocked him backward. "Have you been drinking?"

"No." She worked her feet back into those uncomfortable pumps. "But it's safe to say my dress is sloshed."

A smile touched the corners of his sensuous mouth. "I'm afraid to ask."

Quite suddenly then she began to cry.

"Dovie." Moving swiftly, he drew her into his arms. "What's the matter?"

She shook her head, feeling miserable.

Nick cupped her chin with a commanding hand and kissed her tear-streaked face, tasting salt and roses and maybe her mascara. "You know I can't see you shaking your head, so tell me what's wrong."

Finally she blurted it out. "They're all so beautiful, and they can take care of you and I can't."

As he rocked her back and forth, silently encouraging her to continue, he became aware of a resonance deep inside him, a sense of rightness that he didn't even try to understand.

"I'm just a burden," she sobbed against his shirtfront. "Falling in the river and tripping over your fly rod and spilling wine on my new dress in front of your friends. And I never can think of anything to say at parties!"

He stroked her bare back, her shoulder, amazed anew by the delicacy of her bones. "Don't you realize you're more beautiful than all the others combined? I know because I have my own way of measuring. And damned if I want any woman mothering me."

With shaking hands she reached up and removed his sunglasses.

He drew back a bit when she put them in his pocket. "What are you doing?"

"You'll see." She pressed both palms against his lean, deeply tanned cheeks, loving the feel of him, and brought his face down to hers. When their mouths were but a whisper apart she murmured, "Thank you."

His body sprang to life as her lips brushed his, and his breath scraped harshly when she withdrew. "You're welcome."

Dovie ducked her head self-consciously and wiped her eyes. Finding her fingers smeared with mascara, she grimaced. "Yech! I must look a mess."

Nick dropped a kiss on her hair. "Not to me."

"Is that supposed to make me feel better?" she asked teasingly as she grabbed some tissues from the boutique-sized box that sat on the library table and removed the rest of her carefully applied makeup.

"You know what they say." He shrugged nonchalantly. "Beauty is in the eye of the beholder."

"Remind me to introduce you to my ophthalmologist."

His rich laugher played counterpoint to the tinkle of a piano. As the music wafted in more loudly from the living room, he caught her hand and led her out the door. "Let's go."

"Home?" she asked hopefully.

"Dancing."

She stopped dead in her tracks. "But I don't know how to dance."

"Then it's time you learned."

"Please . . ." Her voice held the same plaintive tremor as the musical notes that haunted the hallway. "Not in front of all those people."

Without another word Nick pulled her into the circle of his arms, holding her in the traditional waltz position. As he drew her into his rhythm, her spine went rigid beneath his hand, and it took all his self-control not to smile. "Lesson number one: Relax."

"Right." She released a pent-up breath.

"Lesson number two . . ." He brought his hand up from her waistline and increased the pressure on her back until the full mounds of her breasts were flattened against his chest. "Now, follow my lead."

Dovie felt awkward and graceful both at once, as her lower body instinctively molded itself to his. Her feet were killing her, and she knew she looked a fright. Gradually, though, her awareness of this man blotted out all other thoughts, sounds, sights.

And as they glided around the hallway as if they'd been designed to flow together, she decided that whoever said fairy tales can come true must have danced with Nick.

Seven

"Pleased to make your acquaintance, Dr. Monroe." The greengrocer gave him an energetic handshake, though Nick could feel the bulbous charge of arthritis in every joint.

Dovie set a dozen oranges, a bunch of bananas, and a pound of pecans on the bleached-maple counter top. "Have you got my freshly grated coconut, Charlie?"

"Bagged it special just this morning, as a matter of fact." He shuffled off to the back room and returned with a small plastic sackful. "Now, what else can I do you for?"

"Let's see . . ." Dovie checked her shopping list, trying to make sure she had all the ingredients for ambrosia. She'd abandoned the idea of having trout for her Christmas dinner and settled on the more traditional Smithfield ham and beaten biscuits, with the usual trimmings.

When the bell above the door jangled she looked up in idle curiosity, then dropped to her knees to greet the two incoming children. "Rachel! Rebecca!"

"Aunt Granny!" they squealed in unison. Their rubber-soled galoshes flapped against the oaken floor as they ran straight into her open arms.

"Oh, I've missed you little devils!" Dovie loved her nieces as dearly as if they were her own, and it grieved her no end that her brother Jack hadn't asked her to baby-sit lately. "What are you doing here?"

"We've come to get carrots!" four-year-old Rachel exclaimed.

"So Santa can feed them to his reindeer," five-year-old Rebecca explained.

"Well, now, I'd say you need some pretty special carrots for something as important as that." Dovie released the girls reluctantly and got to her feet. How many Christmas Eves had she eaten carrots till she thought she'd turn orange in the face? Too many to count! She steered her nieces toward the vegetable display. "Here, I'll help you pick them out."

Behind the counter, Charlie chuckled. "Never saw a woman cotton to kids the way she does."

Nick knew damned good and well where the grocer was heading, so he steered him in another direction. "Dovie tells me you're quite the fisherman."

Charlie drew a deep, quivering breath. "That was before I started fading away."

"Ah, the arthritis."

"I'm not one to complain, mind you, but I'm so crippled up that I just ain't the angler I was."

"Maybe you ought to see a doctor."

"Shut down my store, drive a hundred miles round trip, and give a doctor fifty hard-earned dollars so he can tell me to take aspirin?" Air hissed agonizingly through the old man's false teeth as he began bagging Dovie's groceries. "Thanks, but no thanks. I'm already taking so many of 'em now, I rattle when I walk."

Nick could read pain in Charlie's words but realized he was too proud to seek free advice. So he followed his nose to the fruit stand, picked up a paper sack, and started filling it with plump, pungent oranges. "If I had arthritis, I'd cut back on my salt intake."

"You don't say?" The greengrocer hobbled over, shook open another sack, and dropped some large lemons into it. "Now, why would you want to do a thing like that?"

"Because salt increases the body's retention of fluids, which can accumulate in the joints and aggravate the arthritis."

Several shiny green limes joined the lemons in the second sack. "That makes sense."

It did Dovie's heart a world of good to watch the

two men, one all grizzled and the other all gristle. To her knowledge, it was the first time Charlie had ever discussed his condition with a doctor, even though he'd been in misery for years.

"That's not a cure, of course." Nick placed a wide brown hand on Charlie's stooped shoulder, and Dovie understood the gift of dignity he was giving. "You really need to see a doctor, maybe have him prescribe a muscle relaxant and some mild form of exercise for you."

"I'll do that, first chance I get." Charlie laid a gnarled hand on Nick's hard forearm, pulling the comforting palm more firmly against his shoulder for a moment. "In the meantime, what have I got to lose except a lot of pain?"

They turned then, each of them carrying a bulging grocery bag, and started back to the counter.

"Aunt Granny?" Rachel tugged impatiently at the hem of Dovie's sweater. "I asked you if this was a good carrot."

"Oh!" she exclaimed, bending over to examine it from leafy green top to nicely pointed tip. "It's a wonderful carrot."

"How about this one?" Rebecca demanded.

"Perfect," Dovie pronounced. "How many does that make?"

"Eight!" the girls chorused excitedly.

"That's all we need."

Rachel and Rebecca raced each other to the

counter, singing "Rudolph the Red-Nosed Reindeer" at the top of their lungs.

Dovie dug into her change purse as she trailed after her nieces, but Charlie wouldn't hear of her paying for the carrots. When he also refused to take any money for the rest of her things, she closed the clasp on her purse and promised, "I'll bring you a bowl of ambrosia, then."

"Fair enough," he agreed.

"And salt-free," Nick added.

That drew another chuckle and another handshake. "Thanks, Doc."

"Merry Christmas, Charlie!" Dovie herded her nieces out the door, then held it open for Nick, whose arms were full of grocery sacks.

"Will you tell me what I'm supposed to do with all these oranges?" he asked as he loaded everything except the carrots into her station wagon.

Rachel licked her lips. "I *like* oranges."

Rebecca rubbed her tummy. "Me too."

"Well, now . . ." Nick laughed, jubilant and handsome, capturing Dovie's heart as he managed to reach into a sack and produce two plump oranges.

"Let's eat them in the park," Rachel said.

"Oh, *please*," Rebecca added, her shiny, shoe-button eyes wide with excitement.

Dovie left the decision up to Nick. "What do you think?"

He knew how much she'd missed the energetic little girls. And besides, with the sun beating warm upon his face and the snow beginning to melt under his feet, it was one of those rare winter days that just begged to be enjoyed. "Why not?"

"Last one there is a rotten egg!" Rachel challenged.

"First one takes her place!" Rebecca countered.

"Shall we?" Nick invited as her nieces scampered ahead.

A shiver of anticipation skimmed her arms as Dovie closed the back door of her station wagon, then laid her hand in the crook of his elbow. "Thank you."

A homey town with no stoplights and a square of businesses around the courthouse, Spicey Hill boasted a small, snow-covered rectangle that people commonly referred to as "the park."

"Look, we've got it all to ourselves!" Rachel turned a somersault, landing on her snowsuit-cushioned back.

Rebecca did a somersault, too, then stood and brushed off her backside. "Let's go make a snow fort!"

"So much for these." Nick laughed and laid the two oranges on a nearby bench, alongside the temporarily abandoned bag of carrots.

"They'll come running when they get hungry." Dovie moved into the arm he slipped around her shoulders as naturally as a river flows downstream. "Meanwhile, let me show you the park."

"To the west—that's your left—we have the water tower."

They walked in that direction, the afternoon sun on their cheeks, conscious solely of how close they were.

"It's sort of old-fashioned-looking," she said. "The kind on stilts with a conical lid."

A flock of starlings, their throaty squeakings like thousands of unoiled wheels, fluttered helter-skelter into the tall oaks flanking the water tower.

"Then to the north we have the bandstand."

With one hand Nick cupped the back of Dovie's head and pressed it down to the hollow between his chest and shoulder blade as they started toward the structure. With the other he removed his sunglasses.

"On the Fourth of July the Veterans of Foreign Wars give a free concert. People come from Buttermilk Ridge and Turkey Run and, oh, just everywhere to hear them play."

She crooked a finger through one of his belt loops as they climbed the creaky steps. He seated himself on the bassoonists' bench and pulled her onto his lap. She fell into the accommodating nest of his shoulder with a palm resting on his heart, looking up into his face as he bent his head over her.

"Is this where the teenagers come to neck?" The tip of his nose brushed her cheek, cold yet, as were the lips that made a silken exploration of her own while his warm breath created dew on her skin.

"I don't know." Her head moved slowly from side to side in answer to the movements of his. "When I was a teenager, I was too busy diapering babies to pay much attention."

"How old are you?"

"I'll be thirty-five in February."

"And I'll be forty next May."

"I wouldn't be sixteen again for anything."

"Not even for this?" Nick's lips descended to hers and he shifted her weight in his arms, turning her so that one breast pressed against him, leaving the other free.

Dovie held her breath as he slid his hand under her sweater and inched it up her rib cage until at last her resilient flesh was captured within his palm. A shudder of delight quaked through her limbs as he caressed her breast, squeezing, then releasing, repeatedly, while his tongue dipped into her mouth and hers played a circle dance around his.

"Seventeen, maybe," she murmured when he lifted his head a mite. "But not sixteen."

"And how old am I?"

"Eighteen."

"Okay." Through the cotton covering of her bra, his thumb discovered her nipple and explored it until it stood up boldly with desire.

"A very experienced eighteen," she teased.

Against her open mouth he muttered, "A very anxious eighteen."

The blood pounded in her ears as tumultuously as his heart hammered beneath her hand when their tongue tips met again and passed, moving on to dampen the perimeters of their mouths. The seasons fell away as the kiss deepened, making Dovie forget high-school dramas of sitting in the corner praying to be chosen, and making Nick new again . . . whole again. . . .

"You feel so good," he said in a raspy tone when at last they drew apart, gasping for oxygen.

"So do you," she whispered, and laid her forehead against his chin, rolling it back and forth.

"I've got an idea." Both of his arms circled her waist, holding her still. "Let's sneak out behind the bandstand and make dirty snow angels."

She smiled. "Let's don't and say we did."

"I've got an even better idea." Now he adjusted his hips, settling them more comfortably on the bench until his hardness and her softness fit together like two pieces of a jigsaw puzzle. "Let's go home and go to bed."

Dovie felt him, warm and firm, through the denim barriers of their jeans. "Mmm . . . a very *forward* eighteen."

"Wrong." Nick placed his lips against her ear, his voice a husky temptation. "A very horny thirty-nine."

Her errant pulse skipped to every part of her he had touched and some he had not. "If you tell me you're not getting older, you're getting better, I'll bop you one."

He laughed that wonderful, full-throated laugh. Damn, but he'd never known a woman with such a terrific sense of humor! "Would you believe *bigger*?"

"You're terrible."

"You love it."

Yes, she did. She loved the laughter almost as much as she loved the man. Arms that had been denied far too long came hungering, curling around his neck. Lips that had gone wanting for too many years met his mouth, while her tongue delved into its warmth and wetness. Dovie held nothing back. She had needed Nick all her adult life, and, by golly, she meant to have him!

"There they are."

"Oh, boy, the bandstand."

Rachel and Rebecca clumped up the steps, one carrying oranges and the other a sack of carrots.

Dovie jumped to her feet, her cheeks scalding with shame and her legs feeling curiously watery, as if she had just run a long way.

"Cute kids." Nick drew a ragged breath and crossed an ankle over a knee as Rachel sat down on his left and Rebecca on his right.

"Would you peel our oranges, please?"

"We started this one with our teeth."

"So I see." He ran his thumb over the tear.

Dovie watched each dexterous movement of his lean fingers, his square nails removing the skin and separating the delicate segments so expertly that not a drop of juice escaped.

"Are you gonna get Aunt Granny a baby?"

"Rachel!" Dovie retorted.

Nick chuckled and filched a crescent of fruit.

"Well, he got Curtis and Linda a baby."

"Eat your orange, Rebecca," Dovie reprimanded.

"Here." Nick smiled and bit into his segment with his slightly uneven white teeth before handing the other half to her.

Dovie's heart did a drum roll as she reached breathlessly for his offering. There was something erotic about sharing the orange with him. She bit into it and felt the sweetness flood her mouth, her every sense heightened by awareness of Nick.

"That was good." Rachel rubbed the back of her hand across her sticky lips, then turned to Nick. "Guess what?"

"What?"

"I'm gonna be one of the three kings from Orient Are in the Christmas pageant," she informed him proudly.

"That's because they ran out of boys," Rebecca explained as she wiped her orangy mouth on the sleeve of her snowsuit.

"*She* gets to be the angel Grable," Rachel added with a touch of envy.

"Gabriel," Dovie corrected gently.

"I'm sure you'll both do beautifully," Nick said.

"Will you come watch us?" Rebecca asked.

"If I can," he said. "When is it?"

"Christmas Eve."

"During the early church service."

"I'm sorry, girls, but I'll be gone by then."

"Rachel, Rebecca," Dovie said briskly, "you'd better take those carrots home before your mother starts worrying about where you are." Nick couldn't have cut her any deeper had he wielded a scalpel on her, but her tone showed no trace of the stark ache his words struck in her heart.

"Awwwww . . .!"

"Girls!"

"All right."

"Thank you for peeling our oranges."

"And if you change your mind about coming to church," Rebecca said in parting, "I'm the one who says 'Hail, Mary' and Rachel is the one who says 'myrrh.' "

" 'Hail, Mary' and 'myrrh,' " Nick repeated solemnly. "I'll try to remember that."

After kissing their beloved Aunt Granny good-bye and extracting her promise that they could spend the night with her sometime in the near future, the girls trudged down the stairs and through the park.

Dovie felt the sting of tears as she picked up the pieces of orange peel that her nieces had dropped on the floor. Then she swallowed her pride and asked in a strained whisper, "When were you planning to tell me you're leaving?"

On an impulse Nick stood and moved close behind her, placing his hands on her narrow shoulders and his lips on the back of her hair.

"Don't touch me," she warned in a low, intense tone. "Just answer me. When were you planning to tell me you're leaving? Before or after we went to bed?"

He tore his hands away and admitted tightly, "I hadn't decided. But I sure as hell hadn't planned on letting it slip out like I did."

"So . . ." With icy fingers she shredded the orange peel and flung it out across the snow for the starlings. "It slipped out, did it?"

He thought about lying, but told the truth. "Yes."

A thorn pierced her heart. Minutes passed. A deathlike pall hung over them. Dovie stared at the cloud coming from the sawmill smokestack east of town until her eyes blurred. Nick stood behind her, wondering how in the hell he could make her understand why he'd kept her in the dark.

Finally she laughed in self-derision. "Do you want to know what's going through my mind right now? 'There's no fool like an old fool.' "

"You're not old."

A sob caught in her throat. "Couldn't prove it by me."

"Listen, Dovie—"

"No, Nick, *you* listen! I'm sick and tired of being taken advantage of by—"

"Damn it, I'm trying to apologize!"

"How dare you?" Rage swept over her in a fiery tide as she spun and cracked him on the cheek with her palm. "How dare you do everything in your power to make me fall in love with you and then try to salve your guilty conscience with an apology?"

"Look—" Nick reached out to grab her wrist, but she yanked herself free of his grip and ran across the bandstand.

He followed her, touching her more gently now, trying to make her face him willingly, which she stubbornly refused to do. "Don't keep turning away from me, Dovie."

"Damn you!" She whirled and whacked his hand off her shoulder, then raised her own hand to strike him again.

But as swiftly as it had billowed, her rage subsided, leaving only regret . . . so much regret . . . in its wake. Aghast at her own actions, Dovie dropped her hand and turned away, staring off into space, until she had regained enough control of herself to say, "I'm sorry, Nick. It's certainly not your fault that I'm such a fool."

"Come back to Richmond with me." He stood behind her, his wide brown hands spanning her tiny waist with room to spare. "We'll have Christmas there—together—where the wrong noses won't keep sticking themselves into our business and—"

"The 'wrong' noses being my family's noses?" Although she resented his implication, she silently acknowledged there was some truth to it.

The heels of his hands slid up her rib cage with tantalizing slowness. "What do you think?"

She shivered, suddenly feeling the cold, and

crossed her arms over her breasts. "They'll come around."

"When?" He released her only long enough to open the front of his old leather jacket and wrap it around her so far, she heard stitches popping up the back. "The Twelfth of Never?" he asked softly.

"You're not being fair to them or to me." She lurched back and spun away from him, all her frustrations bubbling to the surface. "And besides, my family is only one of our problems."

"Problems we'll never solve if we don't spend some time together."

"What do you think we've been doing every day since we met?"

"Getting interrupted by phone calls and emergencies and little girls," he answered pointedly.

She couldn't argue with that, but she could try and make him see it from a different angle. "Those 'interruptions' were part of my life long before you ever pulled me out of the river."

"I realize that."

"And I can no more eliminate them overnight than I can let you rush me into an affair. I'm just not built that way."

"So where does that leave us?"

"I . . ." Her mind went blank, and she could only look at him, mute and hurting, without being sure of the cause.

"I have to know, Dovie."

"Why?" she asked in an agonized whisper.

"Because I want you."

"But I love you, Nick, and there's a difference."

He knew what she wanted to hear, but couldn't bring himself to say it. So he let her down as gently as he could. "Look, maybe it's a good thing your nieces interrupted us when they did. I mean, it was nice while it lasted—we had a few laughs, weathered a couple of crises, and even got ourselves a little sexually excited. Now it's time to go our separate ways."

She felt as though there were a cord tightening around her throat and she could barely talk. "You don't believe that any more than I do."

"Don't bet the farm on it." Damn, how trite! The least he could do was tell her the truth. She deserved that. And so much more. "Let's face it, Dovie, my life is over and—"

"Not according to Dr. Rodgers."

"You talked to Joe about me?" His voice, low and ominous, reminded her of thunder in the distance.

"He said that even without your eyesight, you're capable of practicing medicine."

Recalling the conversation she'd had with his friend at the Christmas party, she repeated it almost verbatim. "While you've lost the keenest of the senses, your other senses—which are important diagnostic tools—have compensated by becoming more finely tuned. And because your brain isn't distracted by visual impressions, you may learn things about a patient's condition that a sighted doctor would miss."

A bitter smile came and went on his lean, dark face. "How lucky can I get?"

"If you said that to make me feel sorry for you, it won't work. You may not have your vision, but you've got your health and talent and a fine education, which is more than most people can ever hope for."

"Tell me what else you learned during this stimulating discussion."

She hesitated briefly before taking the plunge. "That a nurse-practitioner is required by law to work under the supervision of a licensed physician."

Nick laughed, but there was no humor in the sound, no warmth. "I think I'm beginning to get the picture."

"Now, just a—"

"Well, let me tell you something, Florence Nightingale," he retorted. "You and Joe Rodgers can discuss me until hell freezes over, but neither one of you has the foggiest idea of how it feels to be blind."

"I didn't say we—"

"On the best days—and there aren't many of those—it's like being trapped in a prison from which I'll never escape."

"A prison of your own making, if you ask me."

A muscle jumped along his rigid jawline. "What do you mean by that?"

Inside she was empty of everything but despair

as she turned and caught the cold bandstand railing in a pale-knuckled grip.

Across the street from the park, a little girl wearing a jacket fashioned out of old corduroy rags of various colors stood with her nose pressed to a sparkling storefront window, staring intently at a flaxen-haired doll that was displayed on a carpet of cotton batting sprinkled with stardust.

Dovie's eyes never left that little girl. "The Christmas I was eight, I wanted a doll more than anything in the world. Not just any old doll, mind you, but one I'd seen when I detoured through Dunn's toy department on my way to buy sewing-machine needles for Mama."

She smiled as she relived that magical moment of discovery. "Oh, she was such a beautiful doll, with hair the color of coffee with cream in it and deep blue eyes framed by thick lashes that stared straight into my heart and begged, 'Please, won't *you* take me home and love me?'

"And her clothes . . . law, I'd never seen the likes of them! A lace-trimmed pink silk dress, black patent-leather slippers, and white ankle socks with little pink roses embroidered on the cuffs."

A tear splashed onto her hand. Dovie bent her head and saw the shining bead through blurred eyes. More droplets fell. She wiped them away and glanced up at the cloudless winter sky. Slowly, painfully, she realized the glistening beads were her own bitter tears.

"To make a long story short," she continued in a

shaky voice, "I didn't get that doll. Mama was preg- nant with the twins and Pop had been laid off from the sawmill since late September.

"Christmas morning I found a corn-husk doll under the tree. She had the sweetest face—Pop must have spent hours carving it—and she wore a corn-silk wig and a patchwork dress that Mama had made for her while I was in school. We were so poor, I was lucky to get anything. But I didn't feel very lucky. Oh, I thanked them and I pretended to love her, but that night . . ." She took a deep breath. ". . . that night I cried myself to sleep."

No matter how hard he tried, Nick couldn't swal- low the lump in his throat. Heartsick, he strode toward her, wanting to cling to her, love her, share her anguish and his. But her next words stopped him cold.

"So you see, I've done without before and I can do without again. Even if it means doing without the most wonderful man I've ever met." Dovie drew herself up to her full five foot none and crossed to the bandstand steps. "Good-bye, Nick."

"Where're you going?"

She looked across the street and smiled. "To buy a little girl a flaxen-haired doll."

"And then?"

Her smile turned upside down; her heart, inside out. "And then I'm going home . . . alone."

"Damn it, Dovie—"

"Self-pity is a slow poison, Nick." She stopped on the bottom step and looked back, watching him do battle with himself until she could stand it no longer. "I wish I had something a bit more original to say, but the only thing that comes to mind is that old standby, 'Physician, heal thyself.' "

Eight

Silent night . . .

Except for the fire crackling in the hearth, Dovie's house was beastly quiet as she decorated her Christmas tree. Halfway through, she stepped back to study her handiwork.

Pretty homely.

The problem was, her tree listed. No matter which way she turned it in the three-legged stand, the scraggly little pine looked as tipsy as a sailor on shore leave.

Worse yet, the dangly old ornaments and the vintage lights, some with the color partly flaked off inside their globes and some of the migraine-inducing "winking bulb" variety, only emphasized the gaps between its branches.

Maybe icicles would help. Dovie loved icicles. As a child she'd poetically dubbed them "silver rain."

Now she made a determined effort to separate each clinging foil ribbon from its neighbors and the cardboard it came in, planning to drape it strand by strand until it shimmered. Unfortunately, despite her careful work, the icicles looked like dense webbing.

By the time she finished topping it off with the tin-can star she'd cut out with kitchen scissors some twenty-five years before, she'd decided that her poor little pine looked like the bad dream of a proud gardener.

All is calm . . .

It was her own fault for waiting until Christmas Eve to buy a tree. All the good ones were gone. But when her brothers and sisters had first announced they wouldn't be coming for Christmas dinner, she hadn't had the heart to put one up. And after she met Nick . . . well, she'd put it off, hoping they could shop for one together.

So much for the power of positive thinking.

Goose bumps erupted along her arms. Again. She shivered, and settled into her sewing rocker in front of the fire. Funny, really, the way she couldn't get warm anymore.

This morning she'd crawled out of her lonely bed and into an old pair of Pop's long johns. They were too big for her, as were the clothes she'd pulled on over them. She'd lost her appetite the day she'd left Nick in the park, and the irony of that didn't escape her. Sometimes it seemed she'd spent her whole life battling ten extra pounds. But now that she was within a cranberry-nut loaf of what she considered her ideal weight, she couldn't have cared less.

Round yon Virgin . . .

A log hissed in the fire and shot a tongue of blue flame sideways. Rocking slowly, she rolled her head toward the tree. There was more to that scrawny little pine than met the eye. Beyond it she saw Mama sitting at the dining-room table with a basket of Christmas cards and her pinking shears, tagging presents long after the babies were in bed.

Without warning, Nick's image replaced her mother's, and Dovie remembered his dark hand reaching across the table for her own, his thumb rubbing the back of her knuckles as they sat and talked after breakfast.

Forcing herself to look away, she focused on the leather wing chair positioned directly across from her rocker, picturing Pop sitting there with the youngest child on his lap and the older children clubbed around in anticipation. His deep voice traveled to her through the years as he read aloud from the family Bible. "And it came to pass in those days . . ."

Nick's handsome face superimposed itself over her father's, and Dovie recalled how he'd always claimed that chair as though by right. She found herself listening for his laughter, his next word, his declaration of love.

But the chair was empty and the sound of silence grew awesome. Why should it be that, even though he was gone, Nick had the power to control her thoughts? Dovie turned her head toward the fire, feeling his absence keenly, knowing a bleakness more complete and sad than that which she had felt at the death of her parents.

Sleep in heavenly peace . . .

Peace, she thought miserably, glancing at her mantel clock and seeing that it was time to get ready for the Christmas pageant. Was it possible to mourn someone who still lived?

"What time is it?"

"A quarter to five."

Nick groaned. "I'm running late." But at least he wasn't running scared anymore. And never again. He handed his houseman a big soft package wrapped in brown paper and tied with gold cord. "Will this fit in the back of the Bronco?"

"It's already loaded to the gills, but I'll see if I can squeeze it in there somewhere." Harley gave a snort of laughter as he found a place for the huge square package between two of the numerous presents they were hauling back to Spicey Hill. "What's in that, anyway? It feels like a bundle of feathers."

"Come on." Impatience gnawed at Nick as he climbed into the passenger seat and fastened his safety belt. He dug into his pants pocket and, using his well-honed sense of touch, fingered the faces on the different bills until he found the one he wanted. Ben Franklin. He smiled. "I've got a hundred dollars that says you can't make it in fifty minutes flat."

"Put your money where your mouth is." Harley chuckled as he slammed the door on the driver's side and buckled up. "It's as good as mine."

Nick had lain awake in his tangled bed last night, wrestling with memories of a woman with boy-cut hair and D-cup breasts and doubting the wisdom of showing up on her doorstep out of the blue.

Talk about flying blind!

But Dovie had taught him what it meant to love. To love not because of, but in spite of. He'd been going downhill fast when she'd jerked him up out of his self-pity and made him take a good look at what he was jeopardizing. That was when the healing had begun.

Now here he was, following his dream—darkly, with neck stuck out.

"Let me out on the river road," he instructed Harley forty-nine minutes and a hundred dollars later.

"I'd be happy to drive you up the hill."

"No, thanks. I'll take the shortcut." The rushing sound of the river, always different, always the same, told him he was on the right track.

"I'll be at the cabin if you need me."

"See you in the morning."

"With bells on."

They shook hands and said good night before going their separate ways.

"Be careful!" Harley called after him.

"Don't worry." Nick knew his way to Dovie by heart.

What to wear?

Something with long sleeves, Dovie decided, reaching into her closet for that old standby, the black wool crepe sheath. Her bare arm brushed against the red silk dress she'd worn the night of the Rodgerses' Christmas party. On a whim she pulled it off its padded hanger and held it up in front of her, smiling as she remembered how young and giddy and beautiful she'd felt while dancing with Nick in that softly lit hallway.

Memories.

Laughter as warm as a tropical breeze . . . kisses sweeter than blackberry wine . . . eyes as cold as the Arctic sky. Dovie shivered, her smile disappearing as she put the red dress back in her closet and slipped into the sensible black sheath. Moving to the cheval mirror, she made a moue at her reflection.

Too severe.

She heard her mantel clock strike six. The church would be crowded tonight, so she'd have to hurry if she wanted to get a good seat. Turning away from the mirror, she opened the bottom drawer of her chiffonier to look for a pair of gloves.

Well, for crying out loud . . .

Dovie lifted her mother's long ivory lace scarf from its nest of tissue paper and, on impulse, tied it loosely about her neck, letting the knot lie between her breasts and wishing she had a pretty pin to hold it in place.

Law, how quickly we forget!

Standing in front of the mirror again, she fastened the scarf to the front of her dress with her grandmother's pin of faux pearls and faceted glass. To further soften her appearance, she added matching oval-shaped earrings.

Much better.

The scarf and jewelry set off her delicate jaw and classic cheekbones. Artfully applied makeup made her dark-lashed brown eyes seem even larger than they were, as did her hair, which she'd brushed back off her face, leaving just a few tiny angel-wisps at her temples.

She looked, in short, like a woman who had taken charge of her life and meant to make the most of it. And she had Nick to thank for that. He'd forced her to face the truth, that it was time to stop playing earth mother to everyone else and start taking care of herself. Now, if only he'd quit playing so hard to forget . . .

No!

Catching herself before she could wallow in her misery-laden memories, Dovie grabbed her gloves off the chiffonier and went to find her heavy cardigan sweater. Her movements stirred the attar of roses, which was trapped in the fabric of her dress. In the living room she unplugged the Christmas-tree lights. Then, satisfied that she hadn't forgotten anything—

Who could that be? she wondered when the doorbell rang. Assuming it was a neighbor needing a ride to church, she ran to answer it.

"Merry Christmas." Nick entered on a draft of frosty air, his hands deep in the pockets of his cashmere overcoat.

Dovie's eyes flew to his, and her heart went on an old-fashioned sleigh ride when she saw he wasn't wearing his sunglasses. "Merry Christmas."

"Well . . ." He cleared his throat as his voice grew thick with words that would have to wait. "Are you ready to go?"

Warmth laced through her limbs as she put on her cardigan sweater before taking his arm. "As ready as I'll ever be."

"Hail, Mary . . ." Draped in a white sheet and sporting wings fashioned of gold foil, Rebecca got the pageant off to a good start by reciting her piece perfectly.

Nobody minded that the baby-doll Jesus lay in the manger long before the arrival of Mary and Joseph. Nor did anybody object when one of the shepherds scratched in all the wrong places.

By the time Rachel made her appearance in a boy's bathrobe that read "Dallas Cowboys" on the back and brought the production to an end with a resounding "myrrh," there wasn't a dry eye in the congregation.

During the service that followed the pageant, Dovie felt proud to be standing beside Nick. He cut a handsome figure in his gray wool suit, starched white shirt, and wine-colored tie. When they knelt and bowed their heads in prayer, she knew a spiritual high she'd never known before.

"Why aren't you singing?" he whispered between the first and second verses of "Joy to the World."

"Oh, I couldn't carry a tune in a bucket," she admitted cheerfully. "So I just lip-synch and hope that God has a good ear."

Nick's voice was rich with meaning, his hand on her nape warm with wanting, as he murmured, "At the risk of sounding sacrilegious, so do I."

Dovie's hand reached for his, and in their clasp the heartache of months dissolved, drowning out doubt and despair. How and when she had insinuated herself into that realm of his consciousness called confidence remained a mystery. Suffice it to say that her love filled the dark corners of his soul with light.

After the service they joined the rest of the congregation for coffee or juice in the common room.

"Merry Christmas, Doc." Charlie greeted him with a hearty handshake.

Nick noticed a definite improvement in the greengrocer's grip. "Say, the swelling's gone down some, hasn't it?"

"Thanks to you."

"You still need to see a doctor, though."

"What's wrong with the doctor I'm seeing right now?" Charlie challenged.

A frisson of professional pride raced along Nick's spine. He shook his head and smiled. "Nothing that a few more patients with your blind faith can't cure."

The two men talked a little while longer, mostly about fishing, before parting with another friendly handshake.

Nick set his empty coffee cup aside, wondering as he did so where Dovie had disappeared to. Damn it, he'd shared her long enough! Now he wanted her all to himself.

As though she'd read his mind, she reappeared at his side. "I'm sorry, but I couldn't leave without saying good-bye to Rachel and Rebecca."

Guilt twisted his insides when he heard the tension in her voice. He draped a reassuring arm across her shoulders. "Where are they?"

She gestured vaguely. "Over there."

In his gut Nick began to feel a premonition. "With Jack and Jayrene?"

"Yes," she admitted nervously.

"Who else is there?"

"Curtis and Linda."

"And?"

"Ray and Lon."

"What about Merle and Mary?"

She was surprised he remembered. "They're there too."

Thinking it was high time her family came to its collective senses, he steered her in that direction. "You know, I never had any brothers or sisters."

"Nick—"

"I used to envy the kids who did, wondering how it would feel to have a friend or even someone to fight with living under the same roof."

As though he didn't hear the glacial silence that greeted them or feel the chill of disapproval that iced her skin, he steered her straight to the center of her family circle and demanded, "Where's your manners, woman? Introduce me to my future in-laws."

Dovie's head snapped up as if he'd just shouted her name. "What did you say?"

He grinned. "You heard me. Now, are you or aren't you going to introduce me to them?"

What else could she do? She introduced him. "Nick, you remember my brother Curtis."

"Sure do." He extended his hand. "Good to see you again, Curtis. How's the baby?"

"Fine." Curtis ignored his hand.

Nick thought about offering him a knuckle sandwich instead, but suppressed the notion and moved on. "And whom do we have here?"

After giving Curtis a glare that would have freeze-dried coffee, Dovie said, "This is my brother Jack. I don't see Rebecca and Rachel right now—

they've probably gone to change clothes—but he's the proud papa."

"Pleased to meet you, Jack." Nick kept his hand out, daring him to shake it. "If I don't see the girls before I go, would you tell them how much I enjoyed their performance tonight?"

Jack ignored both his hand and his request.

And so it went, with Ray and Lon and Merle and Mary rejecting him in turn. Infuriated to think he'd met with such discourtesy from her own family, Dovie realized that the time had come for that confrontation she and Arie had discussed some time ago.

"I never thought I'd say this about my own flesh and blood," she said, seething, "but I'm ashamed of you—all of you."

"Dovie," Nick said in a tone of soft rebuke. He could understand her flare of temper, but saw no sense in adding fuel to the fire. "It's not important."

She felt the restraining hand he laid on her shoulder and turned her head slightly in his direction. Then her eyes roamed around the circle of people with frozen expressions surrounding them, and twenty years of all give and no take boiled up inside her.

"It's important to me," she insisted firmly. "I raised them, but I hardly recognize them. And I'll be damned if I'll stand by and let them insult the man I love."

God above, Nick thought as he turned her loose,

what he wouldn't give to see her now! He could actually feel the anger radiating from her lush body. And he could picture her saucy little chin pointed skyward. Better yet, he could just imagine her ripe breasts heaving with fury on his behalf.

"Now, Dovie—" Curtis began.

"Don't you 'now, Dovie' me!"

"We only want what's best for you."

"Then you'd better shake Nick Monroe's hand, brother dearest, because he's the best thing that ever happened to me." When her challenge went unanswered, she rounded on the lot of them. "You don't want what's best *for* me. You want what's best *from* me. And you don't want to share it with anyone else."

"What do you mean by that?" Mary demanded.

Dovie wheeled on her sister. "Who stayed up night after night making your wedding dress? Who sewed all those tiny little buttons down the back and up the sleeves? Who hand-stitched yards and yards of lace to the hem and the collar and the cuffs?"

Mary's mouth dropped open, then closed in chagrin.

"And you, Merle. When your second-grade teacher put you in remedial reading, who sat at the kitchen table with you after everyone else had gone to bed and worked with you until you could tell your *b*'s from your *d*'s?"

Merle hung his head.

"Ray, who cried buckets of tears when you and

those juvenile delinquents you used to run around with took a joyride in the sheriff's car? Then who saw to it that you toed the mark until the judge released you from probation?"

Her brother's face turned as red as if he'd been on the river all day.

She looked straight at Lon. "Who typed your résumé when you wanted to change jobs last year? And corrected your spelling in the process, I might add?"

Lon looked away.

"And Jack, who spotted the 'For Sale' sign in front of that big old house that you and Jayrene and the girls are living in? Then who insisted that you have the house inspected for termites and talked the owner down five thousand dollars because of the damage?"

Jack stared at the tips of his shoes.

At long last she turned to Curtis. "Who found you and Linda lying half-dead in your bed? Who went to the delivery room with her and witnessed your baby's first breath? Who came straight to Intensive Care with the news that you'd fathered a healthy boy?"

Curtis swallowed, his Adam's apple bobbing up and down convulsively.

"All of you have had exclusive use of my eyes for twenty years, but . . ." Dovie paused, recalling the vigils she'd kept. Even knowing she was finally doing the right thing, she felt a terrible sense of loss. "But it's time you learned to share them. And as much as it pains me to say this, it's past time you started looking our for yourselves."

Nick heard the note of tight control in her voice and took her hand. He felt the tremor there and drew her toward him. "Don't push it, Dovie. This is something they have to work out in their own minds."

She started to let him lead her away, then remembered that he'd taken her for granted too. Digging in her heels, she decided she might as well set the record straight all around.

"And *you* . . ."—she jabbed his chest with an accusing finger—". . . didn't even bother to ask me to marry you. You just assumed I would!"

He burst out laughing and encircled her with arms that gave her the freedom to stay or to go. "Will you marry me?"

Dovie's heart soared on butterfly wings as she leaned into his embrace. "I most certainly will."

"How I adore you!" Nick's face changed, grew serious. "There was no light in my life until you loved me."

Joy pumped through her body. "Then that light will shine forever, because that's how long I'll love you."

His lips feathered her cheeks, her eyelids, the tip of her nose. "What now?"

"Let's go home," she murmured.

When they turned to cross the common room, what remained of the congregation parted ahead of them as the Red Sea must have parted for Moses.

Nick grabbed his topcoat and tossed it over one shoulder. "Now I know how vulnerable my patients must've felt when they put on one of those paper gowns."

Dovie laughed as they stepped out into the starry night. "If it's any consolation, Rebecca and Rachel rank you right up there with Santa Claus."

"Ho, ho, ho." A teasing smile touched his lips as they crossed the parking lot through the crisp new snow. "And have *you* been a good little girl this year?"

Stopping beside her car, she tilted her head back and answered in kind. "Yes, but only because the opportunity to be bad keeps slipping through my fingers."

Nick started to make a fresh remark, then changed his mind and caught her hand. His voice went husky with emotion. "You're taking a hell of a risk, loving me."

Dovie looked up to the sky and saw a heaven of rippling silver sweeping from horizon to horizon. Shivers of desire raced through her as the pad of his thumb drew circles in the center of her palm. "A love that risks nothing is worth nothing."

Nine

The Christmas-tree lights cast a Persian-carpet pattern of gold and red and blue and green across the living-room floor. A black high-heel pump, size six, lay abandoned beside the leather wing chair, while its mate wallowed in a wine-colored puddle of tie just outside the bedroom door. . . .

"Oh, no, you don't." Nick swatted Dovie's hands away, then slid his index finger into the knot of her scarf and tugged. When it gave, he slipped the lacy fabric off her neck and tossed it over his shoulder. "You steal my tie . . . I steal yours."

Lilting laughter escaped her lips. "So you want to play games, huh?"

"Yeah." He turned her slowly and, with only his sense of touch to guide him, lowered the tab of her zipper past her waist.

Air cooled her flushed skin as he drew the dress

from her shoulders and arms, then pulled it down so she could step out of it. But his breath warmed her all over again when he placed his lips to her nape and whispered, "Strip poker."

"All right . . ." In retaliation she turned and reached for the top button of his shirt. As she worked her way down, her fingers took leisurely detours over the crinkly chest hair, the firm muscles, and masculine nipples. The hair tickled; the muscles bunched; the nipples puckered. "You asked for it."

"Asked for it, hell." But honey coated his voice as he hooked his fingers under the straps of her slip and peeled the satiny material down to her dainty, nylon-sheathed feet. "I *prayed* for it."

"Come to think of it"—she stepped out of her slip and kicked it aside, then freed his arms of shirt and suit coat in one fell swoop—"you did look awfully pious for a while."

Both of his arms went around her, and she felt her bra go tight, then loose, then fall away. Just as he'd imagined so many times, her breasts filled his hands . . . and then some. His teeth shone in the mellow light thrown by her bedside lamp. "Glory hallelujah."

Tears seemed to gather between her legs when his thumbs grazed her nipples. She moaned his name deep in her throat, begging for more.

Heeding her plea, he lowered his head and lifted her breasts, squeezing them together with soft pressure. Then lightly, ever so lightly, he flicked his tongue from one fragrant bud to the other.

"Nick . . ." she choked out, dying of need.

He felt the gypsy beat of her heart beneath the heels of his hands as he drew a nipple into his mouth and milked it gently. Moving to her other breast and finding it as aroused as the first, he made a satisfied sound in his throat. "Ahhh, Dovie, they're so hard."

"All I have to do is think of you and they get that way," she admitted breathlessly. "It even happened in church this evening."

Nick raised his head and chuckled softly against her neck, but it was all he could do to keep from tumbling her backward and delving into her, deep and hard and now. He wanted to taste her, smell her, hear her whimper, feel her flesh surround his. But he restrained himself, knowing it would be better for both of them this way.

"Come here." In one lithe motion he sat down on the edge of the bed and opened his knees.

Panic knifed her heart. "What's wrong?"

"Nothing." Smiling tenderly, he caught her wrist and drew her closer, positioning her between his thighs. "I'm just trying to slow things down a little."

"Oh." Her sigh of relief rustled his hair.

"I mean, what's the rush?"

Dovie stood docilely while he rid her of her plain cotton panties.

"We've got all—" His hands, sliding up her

shapely legs, came to a scorching halt at the top of her nylon stockings.

"Nick?"

"A garter belt."

She closed her eyes in embarrassment. "I'm sorry, but panty hose never fit me right."

"A garter belt." He groaned again and placed his mouth on the smooth expanse of exposed skin.

Dovie's dormant senses leaped to life, sluicing downward in a grand, liquid rush as his lips penned a line of love up her thigh. She realized then that she need not apologize for her lingerie.

His imagination, already inflamed by the long months of abstinence, took flight. Then his hands captured her hips and he took her with him, back, back, onto the soft, clean sheets.

She fell atop his bare chest, but he rolled her over, breathing in attar of roses as he knelt between her slender legs and bent to kiss her breasts.

"That feels so good." Heat spread over her in swirling patterns as his talented tongue painted tendrils and grapevines on the swell of her skin.

Nick circled her nipples with lazy strokes, reveling in the lick of grain upon smoothness, then raised up slightly and whispered, "What color are they?"

She lifted her head, knowing exactly what he meant, and studied the rigid crests through passion-lidded eyes. "The color of wild strawberries."

"Mmm . . ." He lowered his mouth to the soft

indentation where breast met rib, damning the darkness that hid what he could only feel, as he continued downward.

Her body became liquid fire when he dipped his tongue into her navel as a bee dips into a flower for nectar. "Please . . ."

"Tell me what you want, Dovie."

She didn't know.

"This?" His breath misted her belly.

She wasn't sure.

"Or this?" He kissed the sweet spot just below her garter belt.

"Yes," she said at last on a sigh.

Nick gave to her as generously as she had given to him. His caressing mouth expressed his gratitude for the loan of her eyes. His suppliant lips praised the healing power of her love and laughter. And his nimble tongue paid tribute to all that made her woman.

Dovie twined her fingers in his sable-thick hair, seeking a lifeline as the waves of ecstasy washed over her. The crest came in pure, undistilled sensuality. When it ebbed she lay panting, drained, and yet yearning for the physical union that would sweep them both away.

She opened her eyes to the sight of him towering over her in the lamplight as he unbuckled his belt and slipped out of his slacks and shorts. Tall and proud and naked, he looked every inch the noble savage she had once pictured him to be.

"Here . . ." She sat up and patted the sheet

beside her, wanting to learn his secrets, as he had learned hers. "Lie down and let me touch you."

"You touch me and I'm gone." But he realized she wasn't taking no for an answer when she tugged impatiently at his wrist, so he gave in with a wry laugh. "Ah, but what a way to go."

With an instinct born of sheer need, her hands and lips began to play over his hard body. Shy at first, then emboldened beyond belief by his welcoming moans and movements, she explored rippling cords of muscle, combed a dark mat of chest hair, and suckled two ticklish nipples before sliding lower. . . .

"That does it!" he declared roughly, rolling over to kneel between her thighs again. Deft fingers removed the garter belt that rode low on her hips. Gentle hands rid her legs of the sheer nylons.

"But I thought you liked—" When his mouth stole the words from her lips, she tasted a spice that was neither his nor hers but uniquely, wondrously theirs.

"I like you with . . ." He leaned down to drop kisses on the newly bared hollows below her hipbones. ". . . or without."

"Now, Nick, please."

He raised up, then lowered himself into the warm harbor between her thighs, pressing deep, deeper, until . . . his whole body went rigid with disbelief when he encountered the barrier of her virginity.

"Why didn't you tell me, Dovie?"

"I thought you knew."

He remembered all she had told him and realized he should have known.

She read in his face a lot of passion, a little anger, and a fierce regret. "Love me, Nick."

"I do," he vowed.

Locking her fingers around his neck, she implored him with a sustained pulling motion. "Then show me."

No power on earth could have stopped him now. Their extended foreplay smoothed his way as he delved into her body with steady, unyielding pressure until he was fully embedded in the sweet, snug wetness of her.

"Oh, dear heaven," he whispered into her hair. "You feel so good, so right."

Tears of happiness filled her eyes. "So do you."

"Did I hurt you?"

"No, my love, no."

For long moments neither of them moved. They savored the feel of having found each other, of being one, of having survived the pain of an imperfect world to become a perfect whole.

Her mantel clock chimed midnight as, together, they discovered the magic of Christmas . . . the one giving to the other, the one taking from the other, with as much joy from the giving as from the taking.

*   *   *

For the first time in her memory, Dovie slept past

six on Christmas morning. When she awoke and saw it was almost seven, it saddened her some to remember the patter of feet at dawn . . . the excited cries that once rent the air . . . those wide-eyed looks of wonder when someone's small dream came true.

But as she lay abed with Nick's arms around her as though he were already accustomed to holding her close while he slept, she realized she wouldn't trade all of her tomorrows for a single yesterday. He was her dream come true. And she was glad, so very glad, she had waited for him.

The steady tide of his breathing tickled her nape. His furnacelike heat bathed her shoulders, back, hips, and the crook of her legs. When his warm hand slid from her stomach to enclose her breast, Dovie smiled and nestled contentedly in his loving embrace.

Funny, really, how inadequate the sense of sight was where making love was concerned.

She closed her eyes, recalling the feel of his hair-roughened skin and smooth masculine muscles beneath her palms. The taste of him, like tupelo honey, still lingered on her tongue. His lime-and-clove scent permeated her nostrils even now, while his soft, triumphant laughter . . .

Love at first sight? Her smile widened. Remembering the morning they'd met, she realized she'd fallen in love with him at first laugh.

Dovie stirred finally, slipping out of Nick's grasp quietly, so as not to waken him. Then she snuggled into her old chenille robe and moved to the window.

The light came over the hill as if on foot, filling in a hollow here, pushing out a shadow there, working gradually to bring on the colors of a new and glorious day. Snow covered the ground like a clean white blanket, laying the past to rest and making her feel reborn.

Enough lollygagging, though. This was Christmas morning, and she had a million things to do.

First on the list was a shower. Last night Nick had asked her if he'd hurt her. But he hadn't. Not the way he meant, and not that time or the time after, when he had protested it would be too much. She had practically begged him, and when he still refused, she had made it physically impossible for him to say no.

But as she tiptoed to the bathroom, Dovie knew she'd overdone it. She was thirty-four years old, and some of the muscles she'd stretched last night had never been stretched before. So after she'd soaped and shampooed herself, she stood under the pulsating spray, letting it massage her love-sprung body.

Nick awakened to the sound of running water and the ache of empty arms. Both were Dovie's doing. As was this peaceful, easy feeling that filled his soul.

Contentment flowed through him as he yawned and stretched, then pulled his palms down over his face. On them he smelled the fragrance of her perfume, gathered from her skin like the first roses of summer.

He lay that way a long time, gathering his thoughts. Dovie's virginity had been a shock, but her shy caresses had stirred him more than the calculated foreplay of any of his former lovers.

Memories of the night before kept coming back to stroke him the way her fingers had stroked him to full hardness with her dainty hand. With a groan he kicked off the covers and rolled out of bed, knowing right where to find her.

Dovie twisted around in alarm when the shower curtain slid open. "Nick . . . ?"

"Good morning." He grinned and planted his fists on his naked hips, standing before her in all his glory.

Having raised five brothers, she was well acquainted with the male anatomy. But her body flushed hotly as her eyes traveled the length of Nick's lean, bronzed frame. And a welter of emotions, not the least of which was embarrassment, thickened her voice. "Good morning."

"I love you, Dovie. Have I told you that today?"

"Does three o'clock this morning count as today?"

"Nope." Bold as brass, he crowded into the small stall with her and closed the curtain behind him.

In the shower in broad daylight? Dovie shrank back against the cool tile wall, putting the warm stream of water between them as a sudden fit of modesty prevented her from meeting him halfway.

Sensing her shyness and knowing the reason for it, Nick leaned down and dropped a light kiss on her nose. "I love you."

Emboldened by his restraint, she rose up on tiptoe and brushed her lips against his. "I love you."

He reached for the soap. "I'll wash your back if you'll wash mine."

She ducked her head self-consciously. "I've already—"

"Okay." He soaped his hands slowly, provocatively. "I'd rather wash your front, anyway."

"But there's hardly room for one in here, much less . . . ah, Nick . . ." Dovie's modesty swirled right down the drain as he began lathering her breasts, the circular motions creating an exquisite friction that left her tingling from scalp to toes.

"You have beautiful breasts, so soft and full and perfectly formed." The massaging action of his strong fingers ignited a fire in her loins. His words fanned the flames. "The morning I pulled you out of the river, it was all I could do not to . . ."

He rinsed away the bubbles, then bent his head and took her nipple into his mouth, smiling against her skin when it drew up tightly into a ripe, ready berry of arousal.

She stood awash in sensation. The jetting spray stung her skin like driving needles, while the delicate strokes of his tongue made her ache deep inside. Shamelessly she cradled his head in her hands and moved against his hard body, begging him to fill the void he'd created.

He did. But not the way she expected. He put his fingers into her, bunched, as though tucking them into the bell of a flower. Then his thumb kneaded that magic key, his touch giving her untold pleasure and asking nothing in return.

She shuddered against him, soundlessly and breathlessly. But when his hands slid beneath her hips to lift her and lock her around him, she couldn't repress a small groan of pain.

"I'm sorry." He realized what her problem was and eased her feet back to the floor.

Her eyes flew to his face. "What did you say?"

"I said I'm sorry." He frowned his regret while his hands rubbed her lower spine in loving consideration.

A wave of emotion swept through her as Dovie realized that Nick had swallowed his pride and placed her needs above his own.

"The soreness will go away pretty soon," he assured her as he patted her bottom.

She reached for the soap and smiled. "But in the meantime . . ."

Dovie started with his hands, soaping and rinsing those blessed fingers one by one before taking them into her mouth. Then she treated his wrist to a lick and a promise. Delicious sensation.

Her sensitive fingers felt the slight flexing of his biceps as she traveled up his arms. His male perfection made her want to weep when she massaged his muscular shoulders and hair-matted chest, his taut buttocks and flat stomach.

This was how it should be for both man and woman, she realized as she took the heart of him between her lathered hands. Her touch was timid at first, but his pure animal groan increased both her boldness and the amount of pressure she applied.

"Dovie," he asked, gasping, "do you know what you're doing?"

"No, but I'm a fast learner." She moved the silken skin tenderly, exploring and acquainting herself with each ridge and hollow, until Nick made a guttural sound deep in his throat.

His mouth captured hers at the same time that he flooded her with fire. When the spasms passed he pulled her into his arms and murmured huskily into her hair, "Go to the head of the class."

She smiled and laid her cheek against his chest. Loving him as she did, his enjoyment had heightened her own.

When the water turned cool, they toweled each other dry and went to dress.

"Where're you rushing off to in such a hurry?" he asked as she started out of the bedroom.

"I know this is going to sound terribly unromantic, but I've got to feed my hogs."

He grabbed her hand. "Oink, oink."

She laughed and pecked him lightly on the cheek. "Th-th-th-that's all, folks!"

"Oh, yeah?" He pretended to snarl as he caught a handful of her hair and lowered his head. Since losing his eyesight, he'd found no joy after sex, only a kind of frantic despair. He couldn't stand the thought of that now, of how empty his life had been, so he kissed her with a telling need, a message of just how vital she had become to him.

"Mmmh." Her breath struck his face like soft puffs of cotton when they drew apart. "Can you hold that thought for about fifteen minutes?"

He groaned. "Oh, damn. I've created a monster."

"Last night you said you were praying for it," she retorted, feeling desirable and utterly secure in the smug realization of it.

"At this rate I'll be praying for a speedy death." He turned her and playfully swatted her blue-jeaned bottom. "Go on, Porky. I'll put the coffeepot on."

"Porky?"

"Sorry," he said, sounding anything but, "I meant to say Petunia."

"I should hope so."

"What time is it?"

She glanced at her bedside clock. "Eight-thirty."

"Ah, good."

"Got a late date?" she teased as she sashayed out of the bedroom.

"No." Nick trailed behind her. "But Harley said he was going to stop by around nine this morning to wish us a Merry Christmas."

"Why don't you invite him to have dinner with us?" Dovie carefully avoided looking at her lonely little Christmas tree as she crossed the living room. Usually there were dozens of gaily wrapped presents piled beneath it, just waiting for adults and children alike to tear into them. This year, though, she'd distributed her gifts early so the members of her family could open them in their own homes.

Family . . . Looking back, she could see she'd cheated everyone, herself included, by becoming so dependent on their dependency.

She hadn't made a doormat out of herself on purpose, of course. Nor had she intentionally raised her brothers and sisters to be such big babies. But something in her personality, maybe something as simple as a desperate craving for the attention she'd missed by being the oldest of eight children—

"Knock, knock." Nick tapped at her temple with a gentle knuckle. "Anybody home?"

"Oh." Dovie came out of her reverie only to realize she'd lost track of their conversation. "I'm sorry. What did you say?"

"I said Harley is going to have Christmas dinner at his sister's house in Richmond."

"Well, then," she said, "I guess it's just you and me against that twenty-pound Smithfield ham."

Correctly divining the source of her distraction a moment before, Nick confessed, "I want you to know that I feel guilty as hell about driving this wedge between you and your brothers and sisters."

"And I want you to know that the wedge has been there since I was old enough to mind the babies while Mama cooked or cleaned or did one of the million other things essential to keeping house."

"What do you mean?"

They moved to the enclosed back porch, where she automatically worked while they talked.

"Just that ever since I can remember, I've needed to be needed." She filled two buckets with equal portions of the corn, chestnuts, and powdered skim milk that she would feed to her hogs. "If Mama had morning sickness, which she did more often than not, I was only too happy to play the 'little mother' and get my brothers and sisters fed and dressed and off to school."

Dovie paused and shredded some of the orange peel she had left over after making her ambrosia, then added it to the mixture in the buckets. "And if Pop was worried about money, which he was more often than not, I'd be the one to say, 'Don't worry about new shoes for me; the ones I'm wearing fit me fine.' I said that even if they pinched! Once, when Pop was laid off for a long stretch, I even volunteered to drop out of high school and get a job. Thank God my counselor talked me out of that."

The mantel clock chimed eight forty-five.

"Understand, I'm not saying that my parents didn't love me. Nor am I trying to blame them for my mistakes. They did the best they could under the circumstances—I believe that with all my heart." She took a gallon jug from under the porch sink and filled it with water. "But they were so busy that I tried to get their attention by making myself indispensable to them. Unfortunately it became a lifelong pattern."

Her voice went raspy with regret. "I think it was only natural that my brothers and sisters stopped seeing me as one of them and started reacting to me as a third parent, which probably created some resentment on both sides. I mean, it couldn't have been much fun for them to take orders from someone who was only a couple of years older than they were. And believe me, putting my own needs on the back burner and catering to their every whim got to be a real drag at times."

Water gurgled as she poured it out of the jug.

Nick hadn't touched her, but let her talk it all out, drawing from her the truths that he'd guessed days ago. He'd pieced the picture together by himself, but now he felt compelled to share his single greatest fear about their relationship.

"Are you attracted to me because I'm blind and you see me as someone who needs you to take care of him?" he asked her bluntly.

"Believe it or not, I don't see you that way at all." Dovie stirred the contents of the buckets with brisk, practiced motions. When the mixture was the right consistency, she rinsed off the paddle and hung it back on its peg. "In fact, I realized when I woke up this morning that I fell in love with you the first time I heard you laugh."

Suprise flickered across his face. "You mean—"

"Before I fell in the river," she admitted almost shyly. "Before I even knew you were blind."

Relief poured through every vein of Nick's body. "Dov—" But his voice cracked and the remainder of her name went unspoken.

She washed and dried her hands, then slid her arms around his waist. "All my life I've laughed to keep from crying. But when I heard you laughing after you released that trout"—she smiled reminiscently—"it was almost like a song. And as crazy as it sounds, *I* knew all the words."

Nick found himself speechless in the face of an enormous tide of emotions. He closed his eyes against her hair and hugged her to his chest, understanding what she meant and thinking that if he'd looked the whole world over—

The mantel clock struck nine.

The doorbell rang.

Ten

"That must be Harley."

"You want me to answer it?" Dovie asked.

"No, I'll get it." After touching her forehead in the briefest of kisses, Nick released her and ushered her toward the back door. "If I recall correctly, you were on your way out."

"Wait!"

"What?"

"My buckets," Dovie reminded him.

The doorbell rang again.

"I'm coming!" Nick yelled as he went back for her buckets. "Here. Now, don't say I never gave you anything."

"Hey, are you trying to get rid of me?" she asked huffily when he yanked the back door wide open.

"Who, me?"

"Yeah, you," she said with a suspicious glance at his carefully innocent expression.

He scrambled for an explanation. "Look at it this way: The sooner the hogs get their breakfast, the sooner I'll get mine."

"You'll get yours, all right," she muttered as she marched out into the frosty air.

"Don't bet on it," he said before the back door banged shut behind her.

Dovie made short work of feeding the hogs. But not short enough, apparently, because when she came in through the kitchen, Nick was alone.

"Where's Harley?"

"On his way to Richmond."

"But I wanted to wish him Merry Christmas."

Nick poured them each a cup of freshly brewed coffee. "He'll be back tonight, so you can do it then."

"It won't seem the same, though." Dovie took a foil-wrapped package from the bread box and a serving plate from the cupboard, then set them on the counter.

"What's that?"

"Your breakfast."

"My . . .?" He leaned over and inhaled deeply of the rich, yeasty aroma that escaped when she peeled back the foil. "Mmmh."

"Chocolate sticky buns," she explained as she transferred them to the serving plate. "They're sort of a tradition around here on Christmas morning."

He scraped a squiggle of chocolate off the foil and

unabashedly licked his finger. "Sinful, positively sinful."

Laughing, she arranged the plate on a tray with their coffee cups. "What do you say we take these to the table and pig out?"

"Or we could take them a few steps farther and have breakfast in bed," he drawled suggestively as he followed her out of the kitchen.

"You're incorr—"

She broke off when she saw the mountain of gifts—foiled, beribboned, and one wrapped in plain brown paper—that cascaded around the foot of her Christmas tree.

Gentle hands pried the tray from her trembling fingers and placed it on the table. "Go see who they're for."

But she knew who they were for. And she knew who they were from. Love rose in her like a great hunger. "I . . . I have nothing to give you in return."

"Look at me, Dovie." Nick stepped in front of her, blocking her view but not touching her. "Your love is the greatest gift I've ever received. There's nothing you could buy me that I would treasure more."

She drew in a deep, ragged breath. "Thank—"

He laid a silencing finger over her lips. "We have the rest of our lives to thank each other. All I want to hear right now is the sound of wrapping paper being ripped."

Dovie grabbed his finger and bit it gently. "Is it all right if I throw in a few squeals of delight?"

Nick grinned and stepped aside. "I'd be disappointed if you didn't."

She knelt on the floor, all aflutter with excitement as she gathered the collection of packages around her. "I don't know where to begin!"

"Why don't you start with this one?" He sat on the edge of the wing-chair cushion and indicated the biggest package, the one wrapped in plain brown paper.

"Okay," she agreed, and reached for it first. But before she could open it, the doorbell rang again.

"I'll get it." He rose and started out of the room, then stopped and wagged a warning finger at her. "No fair peeking while I'm gone."

"Cross my heart." But she couldn't resist giving the gold cord that was tied around it a bit of a tug. Then she had to lift it and squeeze it, finding it excitingly light and soft. Like a bundle of feathers! And also there was that piece of tape that looked a little ragged around the edges—

"Dovie." Nick said her name so strangely that she glanced up with a guilty start, prepared to swear on a stack of Bibles that she hadn't peeked.

But the words died on her lips when she saw all five of her brothers and her sister Mary flanking him. Hoping against hope, she pushed the packages away and started to stand up.

"Stay where you are," Curtis urged.

"We've just come to apologize," Jack said.

"To both of you," Ray added.

Lon looked her squarely in the eye. "You're right."

"We're a bunch of spoiled brats," Merle admitted.

Mary clasped her hands together fearfully. "Can you ever forgive us for the way we've behaved?"

"Yes," Dovie said softly, hardly daring to believe her ears. Joy burst through her heart as she leaped to her feet and launched herself at each of them in turn. "Yes, yes, yes, yes, yes!"

It was like old home week then, with everybody hugging and kissing and laughing and talking, and nobody listening.

Finally Curtis broke away and turned to Nick. "If it's not too late, I'd like to be the first to shake your hand."

Nick met him halfway, taking his hand in a grip so hard their knuckles turned white. "Actually, you're just in time to watch Dovie open her presents."

"We don't want to interrupt your private celebration." It seemed appropriate that Curtis, who'd always been the ringleader, now served as the family spokesman. "We simply wanted you to know how ashamed we are that it took a stranger to make us see our Dovie for what she is—a beautiful woman who deserves the best."

"I'll try to live up to your trust," Nick assured them in a voice gone gruff with emotion.

Dovie's heart filled her breast with wingbeats as her other brothers and her sister Mary took a turn at welcoming Nick into the family fold. When the healing was complete she asked contentedly, "Does anyone want a chocolate sticky bun?"

Six hungry expressions came and went in the blink of an eye.

"I'd love one, but I promised Linda that I'd come straight home and help her with the baby," Curtis said with a wistful smile.

"Sorry, but I told Rachel and Rebecca that I'd take them for a ride on their new sled," Jack explained, adding hopefully, "Maybe next year, though . . .?"

"And every year after that," Nick agreed in a tone that made it clear he meant it.

No one else could stay either, so after another round of hugs and kisses and handshakes, Nick and Dovie were left alone.

They radiated back to the living room and the pile of presents beneath the tree. Her wobbly little pine suddenly looked so beautiful, so dignified despite the hodgepodge of homemade ornaments it wore, and she knew it was because she was seeing it through the eyes of love.

"Now . . ." Dovie knelt and reached for the biggest package again, the one wrapped in plain brown paper. When she finally got it open, she sucked in a breath and covered her mouth with her hands as she exclaimed in surprise, "A down coat!"

"Try it on," Nick urged from the comfortable depths of the wing chair.

She did as he asked, running a hand along a deep-plum-colored sleeve and admiring the

attractive quilt-through design that held the goose
down in place. "I look like a purple polar bear, but I
love it . . . really."

He laughed and handed her another package,
which she promptly tore into after she took off her
coat.

"A life jacket!"

"How does it fit?"

Dovie jumped to her feet and slipped it over her
head. It hung on her like a sandwich board until
she tied it along her sides and belted it in back.
"Perfect."

"If I catch you anywhere near the river without
that on," he warned her in that no-nonsense tone
of his, "I'll turn you over my knee."

She sassed him back with "Promises, promises."
But she liked it so much, she left it on while she
opened the rest of her gifts.

Nick's generosity knew no bounds. He'd bought
her a dozen pairs of long underwear made of pure
combed cotton, breathable and warm in the
coldest, dampest weather. A new graphite rod and
two reels, one for spin casting and one for bait
casting, guaranteed years of good fishing. Sweat-
ers woven of the softest wool and a negligee spun of
the sheerest rose-colored silk . . .

Finally only two boxes remained.

"Open this one first." He indicated the larger of
the two.

"Oh, Nick . . ." A strong emotion misted her eyes
when she saw the black leather medical bag with

the words "Dovie Monroe, R.N." etched in gold on one side. "I love it, but I'm afraid it's a little late for me to think about going to nursing school. In four years I'll be thirty-nine."

"And how old will you be in four years if you *don't* go to nursing school?" he argued softly.

She struggled to master her emotions. "I'll send for another application."

Last but not least . . .

"Heavens to Betsy Wetsy," Dovie whispered when she removed the lid from the remaining box and saw the doll lying there.

She sat numb for a moment, reliving the sugarplum visions of that long-ago Christmas Eve and the painful disappointment of the morning after. Then she picked it up, amazed by the natural curve her arm made around it, and touched the soft café-au-lait-colored hair, the pink silk dress trimmed in lace, those delicately embroidered ankle socks, and the black patent-leather slippers.

The tears came in a sudden rush then, blinding her, choking her, as she cradled the beautiful blue-eyed doll of her childhood dreams.

Nick lifted her onto his lap and let her cry, knowing she needed the cleansing release as much as he needed to shelter and comfort her.

Dovie hugged her doll and sobbed against his shoulder, wondering if there was anyone anywhere as happy as she was at that moment.

Eleven

The peppery aroma of Smithfield ham permeated the house, mingling with the spicy sweetness of cedar and bay. In the living room a little girl and her twin brother played with their new toys in a rainbow of tree lights. In the kitchen their mommy kissed Santa Claus. . . .

"Merry Christmas," Dovie whispered against his lips.

"Happy Groundhog Day," Nick answered teasingly before he lowered his mouth to hers.

"You missed New Year's," she murmured when he raised his head.

He remedied that with a thorough kiss that kept his tongue nestled in her mouth for breathless minutes.

Ten years, and they still couldn't get enough of each other.

She laughed throatily. "You taste like chocolate sticky bun."

He nuzzled her neck. "You smell like roses . . . all over."

"Which reminds me . . ." She placed her lips against his ear so their five-year-old twins wouldn't hear her. "I love my new unmentionables."

"Me too." His hands found the dearly beloved curve of her derriere and squeezed it gently, urging her forward and upward.

Every Christmas Eve, which they secretly considered their anniversary, Nick gave her sexy lingerie. Since they were gifts for him as much as they were for her, Dovie modeled them in the privacy of their bedroom.

This year he'd chosen a wispy silver-gray bikini drenched in lace, with a matching garter belt and bra. And last night, as always, they'd fanned the home fires with a fervor that defied description.

She leaned against him and sighed.

"Tired?"

"A little."

He crushed her to him, loving the feel of her compact body against his. Every time he touched her, naked or clothed, he saw stars. "What time is everyone coming for dinner today?"

"Curtis said they couldn't get here until two." She gave silent thanks that the family ties were stronger for having been tested. "And I don't look for the rest of them much before that."

"Where's Harley?"

"He wanted to see his sister in Richmond before he picked Arie up at the airport."

Dovie glanced at the slim gold watch that Nick had given her when she graduated from nursing school. The one and only time it had been off her wrist since then was the day she'd given birth to the twins. "That leaves you three hours and ten minutes to talk me out of ordering that new CAT scanner for the clinic."

One corner of his mouth slanted up in a smile as he reached into his hip pocket, then handed her an invoice that was stamped "Paid in Full." According to the date in the upper right-hand corner, he'd placed the order almost a month ago. "Merry Christmas."

Tears blinded her and made the lines on the ticket bleed together. "Thank you."

Even after all these years, his generosity never ceased to amaze her. He'd encouraged her to become a nurse-practitioner, then agreed to serve as the supervising physician of the Spicey Hill Health Center. And she needed look no farther than her own backyard to see that he'd given her two of the most beautiful children she'd ever laid eyes on.

"Have you noticed how quiet it is in there?" Nick inclined his head toward the living room.

Dovie gazed lovingly in the same direction and smiled through her tears. "I told you when they woke us up at five-thirty this morning that they wouldn't make it till noon."

"Should we move them?" he whispered as they tiptoed closer to the leather wing chair, where the twins had curled up with a storybook and fallen fast asleep.

"Not unless you want to baby-sit them while *I* take a nap," she answered with a big yawn.

They were silent for a moment, each remembering the miracle they'd shared in the delivery room.

Dovie remembered the sight of those small bodies slithering from her womb, the feel of their precious little mouths suckling at her nipple, and the sweet smell of talcum powder when she cuddled them and kissed them. Nick remembered his awe at touching them, counting their fingers and toes, and hearing them cry.

They'd named their daughter Catherine, after her mother, and their son Michael, after his father.

"Penny for your thoughts," he prompted softly.

"I was just thinking how lucky we are," she murmured.

Granted, they had more than the usual problems that married couples face. Nick's blindness still depressed him sometimes, and Dovie could only hold him, letting him feel her love. But most of the time, when they curled up together at night after their gloriously tender lovemaking, she was the one who felt sheltered and protected.

He dipped a vagabond finger into the ribbed V

neckline of her sweater in a caress so evocative, her stomach churned with excitement. "What time is it?"

She shifted her position slightly to allow him better access to her breasts and smiled up at him. He was beautiful, even dressed in blue jeans and a flannel shirt. But in her mind's eye she saw him as he looked best. Naked. "Time for a nap?"

His soft laughter ruffled her hair; his strong hand stroked her lyre flare of hip. "I thought you'd never ask."

Arm in arm then they walked toward their bedroom, both of them wearing the look of love.

THE EDITOR'S CORNER

We've got a "Super Seven" heading your way next month. First you'll get our four romances as always during the first week of the month; then on October 15, we'll have **THE SHAMROCK TRINITY** on the racks for you. With these "Super Seven" romances following up our four great LOVESWEPTs this month and coming on the heels of Sharon and Tom Curtis's remarkable **SUNSHINE AND SHADOW,** we hope we've set up a fantastic fall season of reading pleasure for you.

Leading off next month is **STILL WATERS,** LOVE-SWEPT #163, by Kathleen Creighton who made a stunning LOVESWEPT debut with **DELILAH'S WEAKNESS. STILL WATERS** is a love story that sparkles with whimsy while proving that old saying "still waters run deep." Maddy Gordon works with troubled children, using puppets in play situations to reach them. Wary and self-protective, she also uses her puppets to fend off people who dare to get too close to her. Nothing, though, can keep Zack London away from her. This forceful, sexy, loving man didn't win Olympic Gold Medals by fading when the going got tough, so he isn't about to be deterred by any obstacle Maddie can put in his path. This is a richly emotional love story that we think you'll long remember.

Barbara Boswell's **WHATEVER IT TAKES,** LOVE-SWEPT #164, works a kind of physical magic on a reader—melting her heart while taking her breath away. When feisty Kelly Malloy is teamed up against her will with irresistible hunk Brant Madison to do a story on illegal babyselling, the words and sparks fly between them. Each has secret, highly emo-
(continued)

tional reasons for being so involved in the subject they are investigating. As those secrets are gradually revealed, along with the plight of the children used in the racket, the intensity of Kelly's and Brant's growing love builds to a fever pitch. Another very special romance from Barbara Boswell!

That delightful duo Adrienne Staff and Sally Goldenbaum bring you a richly emotional, joyous romance in **KEVIN'S STORY,** LOVESWEPT #165. I'm sure many of you remember Kevin Ross who was befriended by Susan Rosten in **WHAT'S A NICE GIRL. . . ?** Kevin is now a successful businessman, seeking a model to be the spokeswoman for his product when gorgeous Suzy Keller sweeps into his life. It's love at first sight, but a love Kevin is determined to sabotage. Suzy isn't about to let that happen though . . . and she sets out to prove it in the most provocative ways possible. He may not be able to hear her passionate whispers, but he'll feel the force of her love every day, in every way!

In **LISTEN FOR THE DRUMMER,** LOVESWEPT #166, Joan Elliott Pickart will keep you chuckling while cheering on the romance of zany Brenna MacPhee and conservative Hunter Emerson. Brenna runs a pet hotel; Hunter runs a business. Brenna lives in a wildly unpredictable world; Hunter has everything in his life organized to a "T," including his wardrobe, composed exclusively of white shirts and dark suits and ties. Despite their differences he's unreasonably mad about the woman . . . especially when he discovers a need in her life as great as the one in his! Be sure not to miss this latest delight from Joan!

I've described **THE SHAMROCK TRINITY** before, but let me whet your appetite a bit more by
(continued)

reminding you that these three interrelated love stories are by Kay Hooper, Iris Johansen, and Fayrene Preston. On the back covers of the books we describe the Delaney brothers as "powerful men . . . rakes and charmers . . . they needed only love to make their lives complete." You'll learn how true those words are to your great pleasure when reading these never-to-be forgotten romances—**RAFE, THE MAVERICK** by Kay Hooper; **YORK, THE RENEGADE** by Iris Johansen; **BURKE, THE KINGPIN** by Fayrene Preston. Be sure to have your bookseller save copies of **THE SHAMROCK TRINITY** for you! We believe that **THE SHAMROCK TRINITY** continues the LOVESWEPT tradition of originality and freshness without sacrificing the beloved romance elements. We hope you'll agree and we will eagerly look forward to your response to this "first" in romance publishing. Enjoy the "Super Seven."

Warm regards,
Sincerely,

Carolyn Nichols

Carolyn Nichols
   Editor
LOVESWEPT
Bantam Books, Inc.
666 Fifth Avenue
New York, NY 10103

His love for her is madness.
Her love for him is sin.

Sunshine
and
Shadow

by Sharon and Tom Curtis

COULD THEIR EXPLOSIVE LOVE BRIDGE THE CHASM BETWEEN TWO IMPOSSIBLY DIFFERENT WORLDS?

He thought there were no surprises left in the world ... but the sudden appearance of young Amish widow Susan Peachey was astonishing—and just the shock cynical Alan Wilde needed. She was a woman from another time, innocent, yet wise in ways he scarcely understood.

Irresistibly, Susan and Alan were drawn together to explore their wildly exotic differences. And soon they would discover something far greater—a rich emotional bond that transcended both of their worlds and linked them heart-to-heart ... until their need for each other became so overwhelming that there was no turning back. But would Susan have to sacrifice all she cherished for the uncertain joy of their forbidden love?

"Look for full details on how to win an authentic Amish quilt displaying the traditional 'Sunshine and Shadow' pattern in copies of SUNSHINE AND SHADOW or on displays at participating stores. No purchase necessary. Void where prohibited by law. Sweepstakes ends December 15, 1986."

Look for SUNSHINE AND SHADOW in your bookstore or use this coupon for ordering:

Heirs to a great dynasty, the Delaney
brothers were united by blood, united by
devotion to their rugged land . . . and
known far and wide as

THE SHAMROCK
TRINITY

Bantam's bestselling LOVESWEPT romance line built its reputation on quality and innovation. Now, a remarkable and unique
event in romance publishing comes from the same source: THE
SHAMROCK TRINITY, three daringly original novels written by
three of the most successful women's romance writers today. Kay
Hooper, Iris Johansen, and Fayrene Preston have created a trio
of books that are dynamite love stories bursting with strong,
fascinating male and female characters, deeply sensual love scenes,
the humor for which LOVESWEPT is famous, and a deliciously
fresh approach to romance writing.

*THE SHAMROCK TRINITY—Burke, York, and
Rafe: Powerful men . . . rakes and charmers . . .
they needed only love to make their lives complete.*

RAFE, THE MAVERICK by Kay Hooper

Rafe Delaney was a heartbreaker whose ebony eyes held laughing
devils and whose lilting voice could charm any lady—or any
horse—until a stallion named Diablo left him in the dust. It took
Maggie O'Riley to work her magic on the impossible horse . . .
and on his bold owner. Maggie's grace and strength made Rafe
yearn to share the raw beauty of his land with her, to teach her
the exquisite pleasure of yielding to the heat inside her. Maggie
was stirred by Rafe's passion, but would his reputation and her
ambition keep their kindred spirits apart?

LOVESWEPT

YORK, THE RENEGADE by Iris Johansen

Some men were made to fight dragons, Sierra Smith thought when she first met York Delaney. The rebel brother had roamed the world for years before calling the rough mining town of Hell's Bluff home. Now, the spirited young woman who'd penetrated this renegade's paradise had awakened a savage and tender possessiveness in York: something he never expected to find in himself. Sierra had known loneliness and isolation too—enough to realize that York's restlessness had only to do with finding a place to belong. Could she convince him that love was such a place, that the refuge he'd always sought was in her arms?

BURKE, THE KINGPIN by Fayrene Preston

Cara Winston appeared as a fantasy, racing on horseback to catch the day's last light—her silver hair glistening, her dress the color of the Arizona sunset . . . and Burke Delaney wanted her. She was on his horse, on his land: she would have to belong to him too. But Cara was quicksilver, impossible to hold, a wild creature whose scent was midnight flowers and sweet grass. Burke had always taken what he wanted, by willing it or fighting for it; Cara cherished her freedom and refused to believe his love would last. Could he make her see he'd captured her to have and hold forever?

THE SHAMROCK TRINITY

*On sale October 15, 1986
wherever Bantam LOVESWEPT Romances are sold*

Special Offer
Buy a Bantam Book
for only 50¢.

Now you can have an up-to-date listing of Bantam's hundreds of titles plus take advantage of our unique and exciting bonus book offer. A special offer which gives you the opportunity to purchase a Bantam book for only 50¢. Here's how!

By ordering any five books at the regular price per order, you can also choose any other single book listed (up to a $4.95 value) for just 50¢. Some restrictions do apply, but for further details why not send for Bantam's listing of titles today!

Just send us your name and address and we will send you a catalog!

BANTAM BOOKS, INC.
P.O. Box 1006, South Holland, Ill. 60473

Mr./Mrs./Miss/Ms. _____
(please print)

Address _____

City _____ State _____ Zip _____

Please allow four to six weeks for delivery.   FC(A)—11/85